"See you at home," Annie said.

Ian caught her arm before she reached the SUV. She glanced back at him. The look of appreciation in his eyes jammed her throat. She felt special in that moment, more special than she had in a long time.

"Annie, I don't even know how to begin thanking you for your help."

She covered his hand with hers, the physical connection making everything fade from her consciousness except the man near her. She smiled. "You just did." She continued her trek around to the car's driver's side, missing his touch.

That was too dangerous for her to get used to.

She'd let down her defenses in college and had risked her heart once before with David and ended up brokenhearted. She couldn't go through that again.

As she started the car, she realized that when she'd said, "See you at home," she'd felt as though his house was her home. More than she had at any place she'd been a nanny…

Margaret Daley, an award-winning author of ninety books, has been married for over forty years and is a firm believer in romance and love. When she isn't traveling, she's writing love stories, often with a suspense thread, and corralling her three cats that think they rule her household. To find out more about Margaret, visit her website at margaretdaley.com.

Books by Margaret Daley

Love Inspired

Caring Canines

Healing Hearts
Her Holiday Hero
Her Hometown Hero
The Nanny's New Family

A Town Called Hope

His Holiday Family
A Love Rekindled
A Mom's New Start

Helping Hands Homeschooling

Love Lessons
Heart of a Cowboy
A Daughter for Christmas

Visit the Author Profile page at Harlequin.com for more titles.

The Nanny's New Family

Margaret Daley

Recycling programs for this product may not exist in your area.

ISBN-13: 978-0-373-81847-1

The Nanny's New Family

This edition published by arrangement with Love Inspired Books.

www.Harlequin.com

Printed in U.S.A.

For if you forgive men their trespasses, your heavenly Father will also forgive you.

—*Matthew* 6:14

To all people who work with service dogs

Chapter One

Dr. Ian McGregor sank into a chair at his kitchen table, exhausted after wrestling with Joshua to take a much-needed nap. With his elbows on the oak surface still cluttered with the lunch dishes, Ian closed his eyes and buried his face in his hands, massaging his fingertips into his pounding temples. How did Aunt Louise handle Joshua when his youngest was dead tired yet fighting to stay awake?

With a lot of practice, no doubt. Something he lacked. Ian glanced at the clock on the wall and shot to his feet. The next candidate for nanny, one who had come highly recommended, would be here in ten minutes. He had high hopes she would work out because no one else had since Aunt Louise had passed away six months ago. Ian missed his aunt's bright, cheerful smile and all the love she'd had for his family.

Locking away his sorrow, Ian looked at the chaos around him and noted he now had nine minutes. He snatched up all the dirty dishes and crammed them into the dishwasher, leftover food and all. Then after wiping down the counters, he stuffed all of his four-year-old son's toys and the clothes he'd dragged out into the utility room off the kitchen and slammed the door closed.

Two minutes to spare. He wanted to be outside before Annie Knight rang the doorbell. He didn't want Joshua scaring her away if he woke up from his nap, especially without the rest he needed.

Lord, please let this one work out. On paper she looks great. We need her.

He'd turned to God so many times in the two years since his wife had passed away. There had to be an answer to his most recent problem somewhere.

As Ian made his way toward the foyer, the doorbell chimes pealed through the house. He sighed, realizing that he should have foreseen, after the day he'd had so far, that Annie Knight would arrive early. He rushed across the foyer and swung the door open before she rang it again.

The woman greeted Ian with a bright, wide smile, and he looked at it for a few seconds before he lifted his eyes to take in the rest of her… His mouth began to drop open. He quickly snapped it closed and stared at the *young* lady, probably no more than eighteen, standing on his porch. She couldn't be Annie Knight. That nanny had worked for six years, the past three years for a doctor he knew. She had graduated from college with a double major in psychology and child development.

Ian craned his neck, peering around the woman with thick shoulder-length blond hair and the biggest brown eyes he'd ever seen. Maybe she'd come with Annie Knight. But no one else was there. "Yes, may I help you?"

"Are you Dr. Ian McGregor?"

He nodded, surprised by her deep voice.

"I'm Annie Knight. Am I too early for the interview?"

"No, right on time," Ian finally answered as he frantically thought back to reading her résumé. She'd graduated from high school ten years ago, which should make her around twenty-eight, twenty-nine. "Come in." He stepped to the side to allow her to enter his house.

As Annie passed him in the entrance, he caught a whiff of…vanilla, and he thought immediately of the sugar cookies Aunt Louise used to bake. The young woman paused in the foyer and slowly rotated toward him, waiting.

Ian waved his arm toward the right. "Let's go in there."

He followed her into the formal living room that he rarely used. As she took a seat in a navy blue wingback, Ian sat on the beige couch across from her. The large chair seemed to swallow her petite frame. She couldn't be any taller than five-one. His eldest son would surpass her in height in another year or so.

Ian cleared his throat. "I'm glad you could meet me here. My youngest son, Joshua, didn't go to school today. He's been sick the past two days but is fever-free as of this morning."

"How old is he?"

"Four. He's in the preschool program at Will Rogers Elementary."

"Dr. Hansen told me you had four children. How old are they?"

"Jade and Jasmine are eight-year-old twins and Jeremy is nine, soon to be ten, as he has informed the whole world. I'm sure Tom told you that I need a nanny as soon as possible. My aunt who helped me with the children passed away six months ago and since then, I haven't found anyone who fits my family."

Annie Knight tilted her head to the side. "What has been the problem?"

All the good nannies have jobs. My family can be difficult. My children—and I—are shell-shocked after losing two important people we've loved in the past two years. Ian could have said all of that, but instead he replied, "The first nanny stole from me, and the second woman was too old to keep up with my children—her words, not mine, but she was right. Then the third one decided to up and quit without notice and left my kids here alone while I was in surgery. That was last week." And the seven days since then had not been ones he would like to repeat. Ian had had to rearrange several operations he'd scheduled and change appointments.

Annie frowned. "That's so unprofessional."

"Tom is moving at the end of this week. I know he wanted you to go with the family to New York. May I ask why you didn't?"

"My family is here in Cimarron City, and a big city like New York doesn't appeal to me. Besides, his two eldest are teenagers and don't need a nanny. His youngest will be twelve soon. Dr. Hansen will be able to hire a good housekeeper."

Ian watched her as she talked and gestured. Warmth radiated from the woman across from him. Her face was full of expression, and when she smiled, dimples appeared on her cheeks. She had nice, high cheekbones. Her hair curled under and covered part of her face, which wasn't unpleasant but not what most people would consider beautiful. As a plastic surgeon he was always drawn to how a person looked, but from experience he knew the importance of what lay beneath.

"Tom told me he hated losing you." Why didn't she use her college degree? Why did she choose to be a nanny? Ian decided to tell her everything so she would know what she would be up against. He heaved a composing breath. "Four children can be a handful."

"I loved working with Dr. Hansen's three children. We fell into a good routine. One more child shouldn't be a problem. I grew up in a large family—four brothers and two sisters. I'm used to a full house."

"I want to be blunt with you because I don't want you to decide to leave after a few days. My children need stability. There have been too many changes in their lives lately. Their mother died two years ago, then my aunt. Joshua is—" he searched for the right word to describe his youngest "—adventurous. He'll try anything once. He's fearless."

"Which could get him in trouble. My younger

brother was like that. Actually, still is. He certainly tested my mother's patience."

"Jade and Jasmine desperately need a woman's touch. They can be adorable, but if they don't like you they will pull pranks on you. I suspect the reason the last nanny left was because of them, but I couldn't get the truth out of any of my kids."

"Are the twins tomboys?"

"Jade is, but Jasmine is totally the opposite. That's the way you can tell them apart, because they do look exactly alike." Ian stared at a place over her left shoulder while trying to decide how to explain his eldest son. "And Jeremy is angry. That his mother died. That Aunt Louise did, too. That I have to work to make a living. That the sky is blue. It's sunny. It's rainy."

There—he'd laid it all out for Annie. If she stayed he would be surprised, but he didn't want another nanny starting then leaving right away.

"I've worked with kids like that. They haven't moved through the anger stage of grief. When my mother died, I got stuck in that stage."

Ian studied Annie's calm features, and for a few seconds he felt wrapped in that serenity. She seemed to know how to put people at ease. "He went to a children's counselor, but little was accomplished. Frankly, I don't know what to do next." The second he said that he wanted to snatch it back. He was Jeremy's dad. He should know what to do, shouldn't he? "I've reduced my hours at the clinic to be around more, but all Jeremy and I do is butt heads."

A light danced in the young woman's eyes. She leaned forward, clasping her hands and resting her elbows on the arms of the chair. "There will be a period of adjustment with any new nanny, but I don't run from problems. I like challenges. They make me dig in. They make life interesting."

Ian would be trusting Annie with his children, so he needed to trust her with all the background on his eldest child. "I should warn you, Jeremy is also having trouble at school. He never talks about his mom like Jade and Jasmine do. They are always asking me to tell them stories about Zoe and me. Whenever they start talking about her, Jeremy leaves the room—or rather, stomps away. I'm at my wits' end." For three months he'd been thinking that, but now he'd spoken it out loud to another person. The very act made some of his stress dissolve.

"Counseling is good, but sometimes you need to be with a child outside an office to understand what's really going on. I'll do my best to help Jeremy."

When Annie said those words, Ian felt hope for the first time in a while.

"I've checked your references, and they are excellent. I know how picky Tom is, and he never would have recommended you if you weren't good. Do you have any questions about the job?"

Annie sat back again, scanning the living room. "What are my duties?"

"I have a cleaning lady who comes in three times a week, but in between there may be light cleaning. I love to cook, but there will be times when I'm held up at the clinic. Tom told me you are a good cook."

"I like to when I get a chance."

"The kids will be out of school for the summer in six weeks. The older ones have some activities you'll need to drive them back and forth to, but Joshua doesn't yet."

"In other words, he'll need to be watched closely," she said with a chuckle.

"Yes. One time he managed to climb to the top of the bookcase then couldn't get down."

"Where will I be living?"

"I have an apartment over the garage you can use. We have a breezeway that connects the garage to the house. You'll have your own place but be close if needed quickly. Will that be all right?"

"That will work perfectly. I'll need Sundays off unless you have a medical emergency, and I'll take off the other time according to the children's schedules."

"That's fine with me. I'll supply health insurance and a place to live. Your starting salary will be five hundred a week on top of your benefits. After three months we can discuss a raise. Is that all right with you?"

"Yes."

"When can you start?"

"Monday. I'll move in on Sunday. I'll have my family help me."

Only four days away. "Great. Will you share Sunday-night dinner with us so I can introduce you to the children? I'm cooking."

"I think that will be a good way for me to meet them. A school day is always hectic with everyone trying to get where they need to be."

"I have a Ford Explorer you'll use to drive the children. It'll be at your disposal at all times." Ian rose. "Let me give you a tour of my house, then the apartment, before you leave. I'm afraid it was a mess from the last nanny. The guy remodeling it will be through in a couple of days. We'll only be able to peek inside because he's refinishing the wooden floors today."

"Will I get to meet Joshua before I leave?"

"Probably. When he takes a nap, it's usually only an hour or so."

Annie pushed to her feet, looking around. "I imagine you don't use this room much, or your children are neater than most."

"They don't come in here often. The cleaning lady comes every Monday, Wednesday and Friday morning. She has her own key, so she'll let herself in."

"That's good. If I have to do any shopping that'll be the time to do it. Do you want me to go to the grocery store for you?"

"Yes. I understand you did that for Tom and his wife."

Annie nodded as she followed Ian into the dining room. "If you plan some meals, you can add what you need to my list. With such a large family, I'll probably have to go twice a week."

When Ian walked into the kitchen, he swept his arm wide. "Right before you came, this place was a disaster." He crossed to the dishwasher and opened it. "I'll have to empty this and refill it properly after you leave."

She laughed, a light musical sound that filled the room.

Ian went to the utility room and swung open the door. "This is where I stuck all the mess I couldn't take care of. I didn't want to scare you away."

"Then, why are you showing me now?"

He smiled. "Because I believed you when you said you like a challenge."

"I don't scare easily." Annie chuckled.

"Good. The nanny who stole from me used to hide the mess rather than pick up. Sadly, I copied that method." Ian gestured toward a door at the other end of the utility room. "That leads to the short breezeway and garage."

The next place Ian showed her was the huge den. "This is where the family hangs out the most." He indicated the room full of comfortable navy-blue-and-tan couches, a game table, a big-screen TV and several plush chairs with ottomans.

"I can see kids relaxing and enjoying themselves in here."

"The only other room downstairs is my home office." Ian pointed to the closed door across from the den then headed for the staircase. "On the second floor I have six bedrooms. I had the first nanny staying in Aunt Louise's room, but my kids got upset. I quickly renovated the area over the garage, but she was fired before she had a chance to move into the apartment."

"Those women give the nannies of this world a bad name. The ones I've gotten to know love children and go above and beyond."

At the last room at the end of the hallway, Ian

stopped and gestured. "This is Joshua's bedroom. I'm surprised he isn't up, but he's been getting over a virus or—" He eased open the door to find his son drawing on the wall.

After church on Sunday, Annie joined her large family at her twin sister Amanda's house for the noon meal. When not working, Annie spent a lot of time with her twin. Annie had been thrilled when Amanda had married Ben last year. Amanda would be a great mother, and Annie knew her sister wanted children.

The day was gorgeous with the temperature around seventy degrees and not a cloud in the sky. Annie made her way around back where her father stood talking with Ben at the grills, flipping hamburgers. With his thinning blond hair and the deep laugh lines crinkling at the corners of his brown eyes, Dad was no doubt telling her brother-in-law another Amanda and Annie escapade from childhood.

The scent of ground beef saturated the air and Annie's stomach rumbled. She scanned the yard, enjoying the sound of merriment from the children playing on the elaborate swing set. Her twin might not have children yet, but she spoiled her nieces and nephews.

"Ah, it's about time you arrived," Amanda said as she put a Band-Aid on the youngest child's knee. "We're almost ready to eat. What took you so long?" She rose as her nephew ran back to play with the others.

"I went back to the house to say goodbye to the Hansen family. The moving van will come tomorrow. They were heading to the airport when I left."

"Aren't we supposed to help you move later today?" Her dad laid the spatula on the plate for the burgers and turned toward her. "Is everything boxed up?"

Annie nodded. "Ben and Charlie's trucks should be enough for the small pieces of furniture I have. After we empty my suite of rooms at the Hansen house, I'll lock up and we'll go to Dr. McGregor's. Then the hard work starts. There are stairs on the side of the garage that we'll have to climb with all the boxes."

Her youngest brother, twenty-year-old Charlie, came out of the house and clapped her on the back. "Remember, you promised me my favorite pie for helping. I've been thinking about that for days." He rubbed his stomach in a circular motion.

"I'll bake you an apple pie this week."

Charlie's dark eyebrows shot straight up. "Apple? Bah! Double-chocolate fudge is the only one I'll accept." Then he said to Ben, "I've been sent to find out when we're going to eat."

Ben pressed the spatula down on each patty. "One minute, so get the kids to wash up inside."

As Charlie corralled the children and headed for the house with them, her dad chuckled. "Get ready for the onslaught."

Annie stood back with Amanda as ten children from the ages of three to fourteen invaded the deck, all talking at the same time. The other day Dr. McGregor had wondered if she could handle looking out for four children, but Annie was usually the one assigned to keep her nieces and nephews in line or make sure the older ones kept an eye on the younger ones because Annie enjoyed helping with them.

Her gaze drifted to Amanda, an exact replica of Annie, although her twin usually wore her long blond hair pulled up in a ponytail. She doubted there was anything Jade and Jasmine could pull that she and Amanda hadn't tried years ago. They had never fooled her parents, but they had confused a couple of their teachers when they exchanged places in each other's classes. Now they went out of their way to be different.

Annie herded the kids into a line so they could fill their plates with hamburgers, coleslaw and fruit salad while Amanda and Samantha, who was married to her eldest brother,

Ken, helped the two youngest children with their food.

As Annie's nieces and nephews sat at their table, she arranged older ones to be near younger ones. "Let's pray. Carey, do you want to say the prayer?"

"Yes," her ten-year-old niece said, then bowed her head. "Bless this food and, Lord, please don't let it rain tomorrow on my soccer game."

When the children dug into their meal, Annie went to make a plate for herself. As she dished up an extra helping of coleslaw, she glanced at the lettuce for the burger. The green reminded her of the color of Dr. McGregor's eyes, except his had a sparkle in their depths, especially toward the end of their conversation about his kids. She'd felt his relief that he'd told her everything about them and she hadn't declined the job. He didn't understand—instead of frightening her off, he'd intrigued her. Annie had decided years ago to help children in need, and Jeremy needed her whether he knew it or not. The Hansens' middle daughter had, too, at one time, but now she was fourteen and growing up to be a mature young lady.

"You haven't told me much about your new position," Amanda said when she joined

Annie at the end of the food line. "What's your boss like?"

"He seems a little overwhelmed at the moment."

"Four children will do that."

"More than that. He lost his wife and then his aunt, who was assisting him with the kids. All in two years' time."

Amanda gave her a long, assessing look. "Sounds as though you want to do more than help the children."

"Any kind of loss can be hard to get over. I don't think Dr. McGregor's even had time to think about either his wife or aunt. He's had his hands full."

"You got all of that from an hour interview?"

Annie started for the adult table. "Well, not exactly. I asked Tom and his wife about him. I have a nurse friend at the hospital where he does surgery. She told me some things, too."

One perfectly arched eyebrow rose. "It sounds as though you also checked his references."

"I could be working for him for quite a while—his youngest is four years old. I discovered that his colleagues respect him as a surgeon, but what I particularly like about him is that he spends some of his time at a free clinic for children, fixing things like cleft palates. Tom told me Dr. McGregor has had to reduce his regular work time because of his trouble with the nannies, but he didn't decrease his hours at the free clinic."

Seated at the table, Amanda leaned close to Annie. "So he's a plastic surgeon. Maybe you should talk to him about your situation."

Annie gripped her fork and whispered, "No. I was told there's nothing else that can be done."

"That was fourteen years ago. Methods are bound to be better now."

"I don't have the money. The last operation nearly cost Dad his house. I can't do that again. I'll live with the scars. I have for over fourteen years. Besides, the fire wouldn't have happened if I hadn't left the candle burning when I went to sleep."

Tears filled Annie's eyes. She'd forgotten about the candle that day at the cabin because she'd been too busy moping and missing her boyfriend.

The memory of that day when she had been fifteen and the family had been staying at their grandparents' cabin on Grand Lake inundated her with feelings of regret. The fire that had destroyed the vacation home had also nearly killed her when a burning beam had pinned her down. Part of her body was burned. The pain swallowed her into a huge dark hole that had taken a year to crawl out of. But the worst part was her mother had never made it out of the cabin. Her dad had managed to get to Annie, but when he'd tried to go back in, the building had been engulfed in flames.

"You have four brothers and two sisters who can help you with the money. We all have jobs. Even Charlie works, and he's still in college."

"He has to pay for his classes. And each of you has a family to support and your own expenses. Amanda, let this go before I get up and leave."

Amanda harrumphed. "You're stubborn."

"So are you. Remember, I know you better than anyone, probably even Ben."

Amanda narrowed her brown eyes. "And the same goes for me. Annie, it was an accident. The family doesn't blame you for Mom's death. You need to forgive yourself and let the past go or you'll never have the life the Lord wants for you. When are you going to figure that out?" Her twin raised her voice above a whisper.

"Annie, what do you need to figure out?" her father asked from the other side of the table.

"Nothing, Dad. Amanda and I are just arguing."

"What's new?" Ken, her older brother who sat across from Annie, picked up his hamburger to take a bite. "Ouch! Which one of you kicked me?"

The twins pointed at each other.

Emotions clashed inside Annie when she turned into the McGregors' driveway and drove to the large white stone house set back from the road on the outskirts of Cimarron City, Oklahoma. She was excited for a new opportunity to help children in need, but it had been several years since she'd been challenged with a grieving child. The Hansen kids' drama had been normal teenager or preteen stuff for quite some time. What if she'd lost her touch?

Annie glanced in her rearview mirror and saw her brothers' vehicles at the entrance of the driveway. Parking in front of a three-car garage, she inhaled a deep breath, then climbed from her red Honda, hefted a large box with her pots and pans from the backseat and headed toward the stairs on the side. Dr. McGregor had told her yesterday he would leave the apartment unlocked.

She carefully started her climb up the steps, her view partially blocked by the carton. A giggle from above drifted to her. She lowered the box and gasped.

Grinning at her, Joshua stood on top of the

upstairs railing wearing a red cape that flapped in the breeze.

"I have special powers. I can fly." The four-year-old spread his arms wide as though he was going to demonstrate.

"Don't!" Annie shouted as Joshua wobbled.

Chapter Two

I shouldn't have shouted. Annie sucked in a breath.

Joshua regained his balance.

Heart thumping, Annie dropped the box on the stairs, jumped over the cardboard box and scrambled up the steps. "Joshua, it's great to see you again," she said in the calmest voice she could muster. "I sure could use a big, strong superhero like you to help me bring my stuff upstairs. How about it?"

By the time she reached the landing, the four-year-old had turned his body so he could see her better, but the motion caused him to wobble again on the six-inch-wide railing. He flapped his arms to catch his balance. This time, Annie lunged toward him as an ear-piercing scream from below split the air.

She grasped his ankle as the little boy fell

backward and held his leg with both hands. Annie leaned over the railing as she heard footsteps behind her and the wailing sound still coming from the bottom of the stairs. While Joshua dangled two stories above the ground, someone pounded up the steps.

Muscular arms came around her and gripped Joshua. "I've got him. Let him go, and I'll bring him up."

Relief washed over her as she released her fingers. Annie dropped down between Dr. McGregor's arms and moved to the side so he could hoist his son up to the landing. While she watched, she took deep, fortifying breaths to calm her racing heartbeat.

Giggling, Joshua hugged his dad. "That was fun. Can I do it again?"

"No." Thunder descended over Dr. McGregor's features as he put down his son and glanced at Annie. "Thanks. One second he was playing in the den and the next he was gone. I figured he'd come out here since I told him to give you and your family time to unload your possessions." He picked up Joshua and held him tight as though afraid the child would somehow wiggle free and try again to fly from the railing. "Young man, you and I are going to have a talk in the house about following directions."

"But, Dad, I wanna help Annie. That's why I'm here wearing my cape."

The first time Joshua had seen her when he had awakened from his nap a few days ago, he'd called her Annie, which was fine with her, but Dr. Hansen and his wife had insisted on "Miss Annie" when she'd worked for them. She was quickly sensing the McGregors' household was much more laid back.

Her employer started down the stairs. "I'll return in a while, Annie. And by the way, you can call me Ian."

As her brothers mounted the steps with boxes, including the one she'd dropped, and furniture, she watched Ian and Joshua exchange a few words with Ken and Charlie, then disappear around the corner followed by a little girl, who had to have been the one who'd screamed.

"That one is going to be a handful." Ken waited for her to open the door. "Reminds me of someone I know." Her eldest brother looked pointedly at Charlie, who was bigger and more muscular than Ken.

"I grew out of wanting to be a daredevil." Her youngest sibling poked Ken in the back with two cartons he held.

"Boys, let's try to be good role models for the McGregor children." Annie trailed them into her new apartment. "And, Charlie, the only reason you quit, no doubt temporarily, was because you broke an arm and leg performing that death-defying skateboard trick."

The bantering between her brothers continued as they brought up all the boxes and furniture from the three vehicles while Annie tried to decide which boxes to open first and where to put the ones she wouldn't have time to empty today. Annie paused to look at her first real apartment. When she'd gone to college, she'd lived at home to save money, then she'd moved into the homes of her employers after that.

Excitement bubbled to the surface as she walked to a door and discovered her bedroom with a double bed, a chest of drawers and one nightstand. Her grandmother's cushioned chair would look good in here. She checked the closet and smiled when she found it was a walk-in with plenty of storage space.

Then Annie moved on to the only other door and went into the bathroom, a pale-green-and-ivory color scheme. It had a tub with a showerhead, so she had a choice. She liked that because sometimes a hot bath worked the kinks out of her body on a particularly active day, and with Joshua she'd probably have a lot of them. She wouldn't have to exercise much with him around if that stunt was any indication.

When she went back into the main room with

a living area at one end and a dining table with four chairs and a small kitchenette taking up the other half, her brothers stood in the middle of the stack of boxes, arguing.

Annie put two fingers in her mouth and gave a loud whistle. They stopped and stared at her. "Are you all through bringing up my belongings?"

"Yes. We were just waiting to see if you want us to do anything else. We were discussing the merits of our favorite basketball teams and as usual our little brother has it wrong. The Thunder *will* win the NBA championship. If you're from Oklahoma, you have to root for them." Ken shot Charlie a piercing look.

Annie needed a few minutes of peace before she was introduced to the rest of Ian's children, especially after that incident with Joshua. "I think I can handle this. Thank you for your help." She grinned. "Try not to hurt each other on the way down the stairs."

When they left, Annie sat on the tan couch and laid her head against the cushion. Quiet. Tranquil. She'd better cherish this moment because tomorrow she officially started her new job. The memory of Joshua standing on the railing revved her heartbeat again. Then she remembered Ian leaning over her and clasping his son. Remembering the brush of his arms against her gave her goose bumps.

Ian was strong. Capable. Caring.

Annie quickly shook the image from her thoughts. They were employer/employee, and that was the way it would stay. She remembered the scars on her body, a constant reminder of the tragedy that had taken her mother away.

If only I could relive...

But there were no do-overs. She had to live with what was left. She was damaged goods.

A knock at the door roused her from her thoughts. Annie pushed off the couch and weaved her way through the stacked boxes to the entrance. Maybe having quiet time wasn't the answer right now. When she let Ian inside, she spied a very contrite child trudging behind his father. Head down, Joshua chewed on his thumbnail.

She wanted to scoop the adorable little boy into her arms and tell him everything was okay, but she wouldn't. Ian's stern expression spoke volumes about a serious talk with his son, and rightly so. But he was so cute with blond curly hair, big dimples in his cheeks, the beautiful brown eyes and long, dark eyelashes that any girl would want.

"Joshua, don't you have something to say?"

The child mumbled something, but Annie

couldn't make out what it was. She knelt in front of the boy. "What did you say? I didn't hear you."

Joshua lifted his head enough that she had a peek at those beautiful eyes that told the world what he was thinking. "I'm sorry. I promise I won't do it again."

She hoped not, but she knew Joshua still had to be watched carefully until he developed a healthy respect for dangerous activities. "I'm glad to hear that. I noticed some cushions on the ground. Did you put them there?"

He nodded. "They're soft."

"But not soft enough to break your fall."

"I know. Daddy told me. I have to put the cushions back—by myself."

Annie rose. "That makes sense." She glanced at Ian and saw that, like his son's, his eyelashes were extralong, framing crystalline green depths. She took in his disheveled dark brown hair that looked as though he'd raked his fingers through it when he'd talked with his child. She could just imagine how he'd felt when he'd seen her gripping Joshua's leg, his only safety line. Her heart went out to him. In the past two years Ian had buried two loved ones, and she suspected he was still dealing with his grief like Jeremy.

"Joshua, I'll watch you from the landing," Dr.

McGregor said. "You need to put the cushions back exactly like you found them."

"Yes, sir." With slumped shoulders, the little boy made his way out of the apartment. The sound of his footsteps on the stairs resonated in the air.

Annie went out onto the landing with the doctor. Looking at the ground twenty feet below reminded her all over again about how tragic today could have been. She saw a flower garden with stones around it that Joshua could have hit his head on.

"Thanks, Annie, for grabbing Joshua. I went into the kitchen to make sure I had all the ingredients for dinner tonight. When I returned to the den five minutes later, he was gone. At first I'd thought he'd gone to his room, then I remembered all his questions about when you were going to show up. Something told me he went to see you. I was coming to bring him back inside so you could get settled without stumbling over him. He can get underfoot."

While Joshua wrestled with a two-seat cushion from the lawn furniture, finally deciding to drag it, Annie took in the beautifully landscaped yard with spring flowers bursting forward in their multicolored glory. The air smelled of honeysuckle. She leaned over and saw a row of bushes below the staircase. "I like your yard. Is gardening a hobby of yours?"

"More like a means to keep my sanity. When I'm troubled, I go outside and tinker in the yard. My wife got me hooked on it. She started this, and I'm just keeping it going. How about you?"

"Can't stand to garden, but I love to look at a beautiful one. I'm a great spectator—not such a good participant."

Ian turned toward her, not a foot away, and smiled.

"How about your children?" she asked. "Do they help outside?"

Watching Joshua finish with the last cushion, Ian pressed his lips together as though weighing what he said. "Joshua loves to, but his assistance isn't quite what I need. Jasmine helps often. She takes after her mother, but Jade and Jeremy will do anything to get out of work—whether outside or inside." He frowned. "In fact, if Jeremy joins the family at all it's an accomplishment."

"Will he be at dinner?"

"Yes, for as long as it takes for him to eat. I used to make him sit there until we were all ready to get up. Finally, I decided the hostile atmosphere he created wasn't fair to the other children."

"How was Jeremy with the other nannies?"

"He had as little to do with them as possible. The only one who seemed to get through to him was Aunt Louise. When she died, he took her death doubly hard."

"He's old enough to understand the losses he's had," Annie said over the stomping of Joshua's feet as he came up the stairs. "Can I help you with dinner?"

"Nope. You aren't officially on the clock until tomorrow."

"What time do you want me to come to eat tonight?"

"Six-thirty, and I hope to have the food on the table shortly thereafter." Dr. McGregor clasped his son's shoulder to keep him from going into her apartment. "No guarantees, though. Joshua, we're leaving. You have a room to clean."

"Do I hafta? I told Annie I'm sorry."

"Yes, but it has nothing to do with your room. It's Sunday, and it's supposed to be done before you go to bed."

Joshua huffed and raced down the stairs, jumping to the ground from the third step.

"If he doesn't give me a heart attack, I'll be surprised," Ian said with a chuckle.

But Annie had spied the tense set to his shoulders and the clamp of his jaw as his son had made the leap. "I imagine my parents felt the same way about some of my brothers."

"But not you?"

"Well...probably so." Some of Annie and Amanda's antics could rival her siblings'. "But nothing like my younger brother."

Ian grinned. "What is it about the youngest in the family?"

Annie smiled and shrugged, then watched Ian descend the steps. He moved with an ease and confidence.

Her new employer was easy to talk to. He was nothing like what she had expected. Tom had told her yesterday Dr. McGregor could work anywhere he wanted and make a ton of money. His reputation as a plastic surgeon was known throughout the United States. He chose to stay in Cimarron City, his wife's hometown, and to donate part of his time to the free clinic. Annie couldn't deny that the man intrigued her.

As she entered her apartment, she remembered an article she'd found on the internet when she'd applied for the nanny position. Recently, a world-renowned model had gone to Dr. McGregor to erase the effects of a car accident. Even with the scars from the wreck she'd been beautiful, but once the surgery had been performed and she'd recovered, there wasn't a trace of what had happened to her.

Annie had an hour until dinner and decided

to take a long, hot bath. As she stood in front of the counter in the bathroom, she pulled her turtleneck off. She usually didn't look at herself in the mirror, but her gaze lit upon her reflection—zeroing in on her pink-and-white scars. She'd learned to accept them, but she recalled once when one of her nieces had glimpsed them, wide eyes glued on the scarred tissue, she'd clapped her hand over her mouth in shock. Annie wouldn't forget that look—ever.

The door in the kitchen from the utility room opened, and Ian glanced at Annie entering the house. Dressed in jeans and a black turtleneck, she looked more relaxed since the scare with Joshua earlier. Her shoulder-length blond hair framed her face and emphasized her expressive dark brown eyes. She wasn't classically beautiful, but she was cute and pert. And those eyes were so appealing and mesmerizing.

Suddenly he realized he was staring at her. He dropped his attention to the pot on the stove and stirred the sauce. "I hope you're hungry. I think I went overboard."

Annie inhaled and smiled. "It smells delicious. Italian?" She bridged the distance between them. "Spaghetti. I love it. From scratch?"

"Yes, that's the only way. It's one meal all

of my kids will eat. That's not the case with a lot of food. Their palate hasn't expanded much beyond pizza, macaroni and cheese and hamburgers."

"I saw some hope the last few years with the Hansen children."

"Oh, good. I have something to look forward to. There are a lot of recipes I'd like to try, but I know they won't go over with my kids." Ian continued to stir the sauce.

"I have a niece who is five and loves snow crabs. She will crack the shells and eat them until you think there couldn't possibly be any more room in her stomach. I'm usually right there with her, but the last time she kept going when I couldn't eat another bite."

Ian laughed. Annie was easy to talk to, nothing like the other nannies. Earlier, when she'd caught Joshua, she'd been calm and efficient. He remembered when the second nanny had freaked out when Jeremy was cutting up an apple and sliced his finger. Thank goodness he'd been home to take care of the wound because the woman had frozen when she'd seen the blood then yelled for him. He imagined Annie would have handled it and had the bleeding stopped before he came into the kitchen.

Ian put the spaghetti noodles on to cook then

glanced around to make sure everything else was ready.

Those beautiful eyes connected with his. "Can I help you? Set the table?"

"It's already set in the dining room." Ian swung back to the stove, stirring the sauce when he didn't need to. He had to do something. Looking at her was distracting.

"Do you usually eat in the dining room?"

"No—" he waved toward the table that sat six in the alcove "—usually in here, but this is a special occasion. We're welcoming you to our home. I want this evening to be a nice calm one. Now, if only my children cooperate, it might be."

"The least I can do is help you carry the food to the table."

Ian made sure he had eye contact with Annie then said, smiling, "What part of 'you are our guest' do you not understand? Guests are supposed to relax and enjoy themselves. Nothing more than that."

A grin twitched at the corners of her mouth. "Aye, aye, sir. I've got that. It's awfully quiet. Where are the children?"

Ian frowned. "Come to think of it, Jade was the last one in here. That was fifteen minutes ago. I haven't heard a peep out of them since." He walked to the intercom and pressed a button. "Time for dinner, everyone. Don't forget to wash your hands."

"I like that. Does it work?"

"Yes. Saves me yelling or going in search of them, if you meant the intercom. Otherwise, not always about washing their hands."

A few minutes later, the first to appear in the kitchen was Jade quickly followed by Jasmine, exact replicas of each other down to the clothes they wore. "You two can help put the food on the table. Where's Joshua? He was with you in the den doing his homework."

Jasmine put her hand on her waist. "He was coloring. He doesn't have any homework."

"You and I know that, but since you, Jade and Jeremy do, he thinks he should. Did you leave him in there alone with the crayons?"

"No, he left to go to the bathroom."

"How long ago?"

Jade looked at the ceiling and tapped her chin. "I guess a while ago."

"Jade, Jasmine, this is Annie, your new nanny." Ian turned off the oven then headed for the hallway. "Annie, would you remove the pasta when it's done? I'll be back after I find Joshua. He marches to his own music."

"Don't worry. I'll help your girls get everything on the table."

Ian paused at the doorway, started to tell her

she didn't have to and then decided instead that he'd give her an extra day of pay. He was afraid she would earn every bit of the money and more by the end of the evening. For starters, his daughters dressing alike didn't bode well.

Ian went to the downstairs bathroom and checked for Joshua. It was too clean and neat for Joshua to have been there. He mounted the stairs two at a time. He knew Joshua was still in the house because he'd set the alarm to beep twice when someone opened an outside door. The last time it had gone off was when Annie had come in.

The children's bathroom on the second floor was empty, so Ian made his way to the one connected to his bedroom. No Joshua. He returned to the hall and looked into his youngest son's room. Empty.

Maybe he got outside somehow. Giggles wafted to him. He marched down the hallway to where Aunt Louise used to stay and turned the knob. More laughter pealed. Quickly Ian crossed to the bathroom and found Joshua in the big tub, washing himself.

Sitting in a foot of water, Joshua beamed up at him. "I'm washing my hands."

"I see. Why did you come in here?"

"I miss Aunt Louise. Jeremy was asleep, so I came in here. Is Annie here?"

Joshua's sometimes-disconnected thoughts could be hard to follow. "Yes, she is and hungry." Ian held a towel open for his son. "Time to get out, get dressed and come downstairs." At least this time Joshua had taken off his clothes before getting into the bath.

Joshua jumped up, splashing the water, and stepped out onto the tile floor. "Okie dokie."

Ian waited at the doorway for his youngest to dress himself. When Joshua ran past him and toward the stairs, Ian made a detour to Jeremy's room and knocked on the door. No answer. He decided to make sure Jeremy was there, so he pushed the door open and found his eldest curled on the bed, his eyes closed.

Ian sat next to Jeremy and shook his shoulder to wake him up.

His son's arms lashed out at Ian. "Get away." Blinking rapidly, Jeremy pushed away as if he was coming out of a nightmare and didn't know where he was.

"What's wrong? A bad dream?"

Jeremy looked around him, then lowered his head.

"Dinner is ready." Ian spied Joshua in the doorway and waved him away.

His eldest son clenched the bedcovers. When he didn't say anything, Ian rose, not sure what was going on. "I expect you downstairs to meet the…Annie."

Jeremy flung himself across the bed and hurried out of the room—leaving Ian even more perplexed by his behavior. Not sure his son would even go to the dining room, Ian hastened after him.

Chapter Three

Annie took the seat at the end where the twins indicated she should sit. All the food was on the formal dining room table, and Jade and Jasmine sat on one side, constantly looking over their shoulders toward the foyer or staring at Annie.

She checked her watch. "Maybe I should go see if your dad needs help."

"Knowing Joshua, he's probably hiding. He does that sometimes," the girl closest to Annie said.

Jasmine? They were both wearing jeans and matching shirts and ponytails. According to Ian, they didn't dress alike anymore. Obviously, tonight they had other plans.

The other sister grinned. "We should go ahead and eat."

Annie shoved her chair back. "Wait until the others come. I think I'll go see what's keeping them." Something didn't feel right. She started for the hallway and found Joshua coming down the staircase, his lower lip sticking out. She hurried to him. "Is something wrong, Joshua?"

"Daddy is in Jeremy's room. He made me go away."

She escorted Joshua to his seat across from one of the twins. "Well, sometimes parents need private time with a child without any interruptions."

"Jeremy was telling Daddy to leave. I saw his angry face."

"Jeremy is in one of his moods," one of the twins chimed in.

"Jade, I think—"

"I'm Jasmine."

"Okay, Jasmine. I think we should go ahead and eat before the food gets cold."

"But you said we should wait," the real Jade said, her pout matching Joshua's.

A sinus headache, common for her in the spring, hammered against Annie's forehead behind her eyes. Remaining calm was the best way to deal with children. She took a moment to compose herself then bowed her head.

"What are ya doin'?" Joshua grabbed a roll from the basket near him.

Annie glanced at him. "Blessing the food."

"What's wrong with it?"

"Nothing, Joshua. I pray over my meal before I eat."

All evidence of a pout vanished, and he grinned. "I pray at night before bed."

"We used to with Aunt Louise, but those other nannies didn't," Jasmine said, grabbing the bowl of spaghetti and scooping pasta onto her plate.

"We do when Daddy eats with us." Jade folded her arms over her chest. "I'm waiting."

"I'm not. I'm staaarving," Joshua said.

While Jasmine joined him and piled sauce all over her spaghetti, Jade glared at her sister, then her little brother. When her two siblings started eating, she slapped her hand down on the table. "We should wait."

Out of the corner of her eye, Annie spied Ian entering the dining room with a scowling Jeremy trailing slowly behind him.

"Good. You have started. Spaghetti is best when it's hot." Ian winked at Annie then took his chair at the head of the table. "Jeremy, this is Annie."

"Hi, Jeremy," Annie said.

"I don't need a nanny. I'm gonna be ten at the end of next month." Jeremy's mouth firmed in a hard, thin line.

"Neither do we." Jade mimicked her older brother's expression. "We're eight. Nannies are for babies." She sent Joshua a narrow-eyed look as if he were the only reason Annie was there.

"I'm not a baby." Joshua thumped his chest. "I'm four. I'm gonna be five soon."

"How soon?" Annie asked him, hoping to change the subject.

Joshua peered at his father.

"Two weeks. The twenty-seventh."

"You act like a baby. Look at what you did today. You could have *died* today." Jade shoved back her chair, whirled around and ran from the room.

Annie's first impulse was to go after the girl, but she didn't know her yet. Jade must have been the one who'd screamed at the bottom of the steps earlier when Joshua was on the railing.

Instead, Ian stood. "Keep eating." Then he left the room.

Wide-eyed, Joshua looked at Jeremy, then Jasmine and finally Annie. "I won't die."

The pounding in her head increased. "Jade was just worried about what you did today. Standing on the railing is dangerous."

"Yeah, dork. You have a death wish." Jeremy snatched a roll and began tearing it apart.

"Death wish?" Confusion clouded Joshua's eyes. Tears filled them. "I don't wanna die."

"Then, stop doing dumb things." Jeremy tossed a piece of bread at his younger brother.

Joshua threw his half-eaten roll at Jeremy. It plunked into the milk glass, and the white liquid splashed everywhere.

Grabbing for a roll in the basket, Jeremy twisted toward Joshua.

"Stop it right now." Annie shot to her feet. "The dinner table is no place for a food fight. If you don't want to eat peacefully, then go to your rooms."

Jeremy glared. "I don't need a nanny telling me what to do."

Annie counted to ten, breathed deeply and replied, "Apparently you do, because civilized people don't act like this at the table. It's your choice. Stay and eat politely or leave." She returned his intense look with a serene one while inside she quaked. She might be fired after tonight.

Jeremy took the roll and stomped away from the dining room while Joshua hung his head and murmured, "Sorry."

"Apology accepted." Although her stomach was knotted, Annie picked up her fork and took a bite. "Delicious. Your dad is a good cook." If only she hadn't walked around the yard enjoying the beautiful flowers before coming inside, she wouldn't be contending with a headache. In spring she limited her time outside because she had trouble with her allergies.

"One day I'm gonna be a good cook, too." Jasmine continued eating.

"Jasmine, I can teach you a few things. I especially enjoy baking."

"I'm Jade." The girl lowered her gaze. "Sorry about that. We were just playing with you."

"I understand. I have a twin sister."

"You do? I have a girlfriend who has a twin brother. They don't look alike, though."

"They're fraternal twins. You and Jasmine are identical, like I am with my sister, Amanda."

"I'd like to meet your twin." Jade—at least Annie hoped that was who she was—took a gulp of her milk.

Ian reentered the dining room with Jasmine. "I'd like to meet your twin, too." He scanned the table. "Where's Jeremy?"

"He chose not to eat." Annie took another bite of her spaghetti as the knots in her stomach began to unravel.

Joshua huffed. "He threw food at me."

Ian's eyebrows rose. "Why?"

"He's mean."

Ian swung his attention to Annie, a question in his eyes.

"Jeremy chose to leave rather than calmly eat his dinner," she answered while her head throbbed.

Ian nodded then said to the children, "Tell Annie about what you're doing this week in school."

Later, contrary to what Ian had asked, Annie finished putting the dishes into the dishwasher. She had to do something while she waited for Ian to return from upstairs.

He came into the kitchen after putting Joshua to bed. "He fell right to sleep. Thankfully he usually does, while Jade and Jasmine rarely do. Often I'll find one of them in the other's bed in the morning. They shared a room until a year ago when they decided they should have their own rooms like their brothers."

"I shared one with Amanda until I went to college." Annie hung up the washrag and faced him.

His gaze skimmed over the clean counters and stove. "I should have known you would do the dishes."

"I figured it was part of my job."

"Let's go into the den and talk where it's more comfortable. I'm sure after the evening we had, you have a ton of questions."

Annie went ahead of him from the kitchen. "A few."

In the den she sat at one end of the tan couch while Ian took the other. A fine-honed tension electrified the air. As she turned to face him, he did the same. Exhaustion blanketed his features, his green eyes dull. The urge to comfort him swamped Annie, but she balled her hands and waited for him to speak first.

He cleared his throat. "What happened tonight has been the norm ever since Aunt Louise died. Life wasn't perfect before, but she established a routine and gave my children boundaries." He combed his fingers through his brown hair then rubbed his palm across his nape. "I'm finding it hard to make a living and be here for my children. I've tried to do what Aunt Louise did, but my efforts seem to fall flat."

A dilemma a lot of parents had. "We live in a society that seems to be constantly on the go. If we're not busy, we're bored," Annie said. "A lot has happened to your children in the past two years. This especially affects Jeremy because he's the eldest and knows what's going on. Even to a certain extent your girls do, especially about your aunt's death."

"I've talked to each of my kids about Aunt Louise unexpectedly dying."

"Have you ever sat down and talked with

them all together? I think the best thing my parents did was have a family meeting once a week, or more if needed."

"Sometimes because of our busy schedules it's hard to do that. Tonight was the first time in a while we've even eaten together."

"Decide on what you feel has to be done, what you can do away with and what would be nice if there's enough time."

"I love my children and have rules that they need to follow, but I can't seem to get a handle on it. Maybe when you've been with the kids awhile, we can talk again."

Annie thought of the day planner she'd used to track the children's activities and school functions at her other employers'. She wished her mother was still alive to talk to, but she could go see her eldest sister, Rachel, who'd taken over and helped raise them when their mother died. "I'd like to get a weekly calendar and put it up in the kitchen to help us and the kids keep up with everything. That's where family time can be scheduled."

"I'm interested in hearing more about your family meetings. What did you talk about?"

Thinking back to a few she'd had with her siblings, Annie chuckled. "Some could get quite heated, but a rule my parents had was that no one left the room until a solution to a conflict was reached. Once we were two hours late going to bed."

"So there are rules?"

"Yes, a few my parents insisted on and some we got to add. It's a time for everyone in the family to have a voice."

Ian smiled, and for a moment the tired lines vanished from his face. "I like the concept. After you've been working for a week or so, I'd like to see if we could try that."

"Have your children talked with a grief counselor?" *Have you? Have you let life get in the way of grieving?*

"As I told you, I had Jeremy go to a counselor, but he refused to cooperate. Our pastor came over after Aunt Louise's funeral and talked with the whole family. The same when my wife died."

"How long has Jeremy been so angry?"

"He was some before Aunt Louise died, but mostly since then. It's getting worse. There are times he almost seems frightened. Before all this began, he was the sweetest child, but in the past nine months… I don't know what's going on."

"Is he being bullied at school?"

"I've talked with the teacher. She's noticed he keeps to himself more. In fact, a few months ago he bullied another classmate. That's when he started counseling. So far there hasn't been another incident. I won't tolerate bullying, and he knows it."

The feeling that the child was screaming for help kept nagging her. Was it grief? Something else? A stage he was going through? "What does he say?"

"Nothing. He used to tell me everything. Now I can't get anything out of him. I feel like I'm losing my son."

Not if she could do anything about it. This was why Annie had chosen to be a nanny and why she had been led to this family. "No, you aren't losing your son. If it's a phase he's going through, he'll grow out of it. If it's something else, we'll find out what it is and deal..." Her words faded into silence.

Surprise flashed across Ian's face.

Did the word *we'll* sound presumptuous? Ian was her employer. Yes, she would help with Jeremy, but he was the parent. Not her. "What I mean is as his nanny I'll try to help you and him as much as possible. But you're his father, and whatever you say is what I'll do."

A gleam sparkled in Ian's eyes. "I want your input. I need it. So I think you're right—we're a team. I'm determined, at the very least, to get my family back to the way it was when Aunt Louise was here."

Annie heard the sincerity in his voice. *A team.* It might be the closest she'd come to raising children as if she were their mother. The Hansens had been great to work for and had valued her input, but she'd always felt like an employee. As of late, she realized she wanted more, and yet she hadn't dated much. She was always so busy with her own family or the children she was taking care of.

"I won't be going into work tomorrow until after we take the kids to school," Ian said.

"I thought that was something you wanted me to do."

"You're right, but I want to go with you so I can introduce you to the teachers. If there's a problem with one of them at school, sometimes I can go take care of it. But if I'm in surgery, that will be hard. I don't anticipate trouble with the girls, but there might be with Joshua or Jeremy. I've already had to go to school for Jeremy four times this year and once for Joshua when he fell on the playground and hit his head." He shook his head. "Probably one of many times he'll have to have stitches."

"I like the idea of meeting their teachers. I want to find out what kind of homework to expect from them. That way we can get it done before you come home on the days I'm not taking them to lessons. I find if they tackle it after getting a snack when they come home from school they'll finish quickly so they can play. It cuts down on whining later when they're more tired."

"The other nannies didn't want to help with their homework, which left me doing it late and yes, they usually complained and made the process longer."

Annie tried to stifle a yawn, but she couldn't. "I think it's time I go to bed. Six will be here in—" she glanced at her watch "—nine hours, and I still need to find some of the items I'll need tomorrow." She stood and stretched out her hand toward him.

Ian rose, clasping hers and shaking it. "Thank you, Annie."

"For what?" She slipped her hand from his warm grasp.

"Taking this job. I'm not sure what I would have done. I know you had several offers. What made you accept mine?"

"I prayed about it, and like I said, I love a good challenge."

"You may regret those words."

Would she? If she became too invested in the family and Ian remarried, no longer needing her services, she might. She wanted to care but not so much she would get hurt.

"Dad! Dad!" one of the girls shouted.

He hurried into the foyer with Annie right behind him. "Why aren't you in bed?"

"Something is wrong with Jeremy. Come quick."

Chapter Four

Annie followed right behind Ian as he took the stairs two at a time and rushed down the hallway. He pushed his way between his twin daughters into Jeremy's bedroom. With a glimpse at the bed, Annie knew what was happening. His head was thrown back, his stiff body shaking: Jeremy was having a seizure.

One of the twins grabbed the other's hand, tears running down both girls' faces. "What's wrong with Jeremy?"

Annie herded them away from the door and closed it behind her. Jeremy was in good hands with his father being a doctor, but right now the twins were scared and upset. Trying to decide what to tell them, Annie drew them away from the room a few yards before the one dressed in a nightgown jerked away.

"What's wrong?" the child shouted at Annie.

The other girl threw herself at Annie, wrapping her arms around her and clinging to her. "Is he going to die?"

"No, Jeremy will be fine. Your dad is helping him." Annie forced calmness into her voice to counter the twins' raising panic. Since Ian had never told her about the seizures, this must be the first one. She'd gone to school with a friend who'd had epilepsy, and Annie had learned to deal with the episodes when they happened. Some of her classmates had steered clear of Becca because of that, but she hadn't. Becca had needed friends more than ever.

The twin who wore the nightgown pointed toward her brother's bedroom, her arm quavering as much as Jeremy had been. "No, he's not. His eyes rolled back."

The door opened and Ian stood in the entrance, his attention switching back and forth between the girls and Annie. "Your brother will be all right. He had a seizure, which makes him act differently for a short time, but he's falling asleep now, and you all need to go to bed, too. You have school tomorrow."

"But, Dad—" the twin wearing the nightgown said.

"Jasmine, this is not the time to argue."

Annie clasped both girls' shoulders. "Would

it be okay if they peek in and see for themselves that Jeremy is fine now?"

Ian glanced at her, and he nodded. "Quietly. Then to bed."

Annie walked with them and peered into the bedroom. Jeremy's eyes were closed and his body was still, relaxed. "See? After a seizure a lot of people are really tired and will sleep."

Jade slanted a look at Annie. "Will he have another one?"

"I'll be here if he does," Ian answered then leaned over and kissed the tops of his daughters' heads. "Good night. Love you two."

After the twins hugged their dad, Annie gently guided them toward their end of the hall. When both entered Jade's room, Annie didn't say anything to them. Given what they witnessed, they'd probably start the night together.

"Have you two brushed your teeth?"

"Yes," they said together.

"Do you have your clothes laid out for school tomorrow?"

They looked at each other then at Annie as if she'd grown another head. Jasmine said, "No, why would we do that? I never know what I feel like wearing until I get up."

Jade glanced at her closet. "Well, actually I do know. The same thing I always do, jeans and a shirt. So I guess I could."

Jasmine jerked her thumb toward her sister. "She wears boring clothes. I don't, and my mood makes a difference."

Jade charged to her closet and yanked down a shirt and tossed it on a chair where a pair of jeans lay. "And that's why we're always late."

Before war was declared, Annie stepped between the twins. "We won't be late tomorrow. Jasmine, do I need to wake you up fifteen minutes early so you can pick out your clothes?"

"No! I need my beauty sleep." A serious look descended on Jasmine's face.

Annie nearly laughed but bit the inside of her mouth to keep from doing it. These twins were polar opposites. Even if they dressed alike, their behavior would give them away eventually. At least Amanda and she were similar in personalities, especially when they were young, which made it easier to change identities.

"Fine. We'll be leaving on time so you'll need to be ready. I won't make the others late because you are."

Jasmine's eyes grew round. "Dad won't like that."

Annie smiled. "Be on time and there won't be a problem."

"What about Jeremy? What if that happens on the way to school?" Jade asked, drawing Annie's attention away from her sister.

"Again, don't worry. We'll deal with what happens at the time. My mom used to say we shouldn't borrow stress by worrying. What we fear might never happen." Annie paused a few seconds to let that bit of wisdom sink in then added, "Time for bed. Have you said your prayers?"

Jade shook her head. "But we will. Jeremy needs our help."

"Yes, he can always use your prayers." Annie stood back while the twins walked to the double bed.

The two girls knelt and went through a list of people to bless. At the end Jasmine said, "God, please fix my brother. Amen."

When they hopped up, Jade crawled across the bed to the other side while Jasmine settled on the right. Annie moved to the doorway and switched off the overhead light.

"Good night, girls."

Jasmine turned on the bedside lamp then pulled the covers up over her shoulders, saying, "I need a light on to go to sleep," while Jade murmured, "Good night."

"Door open or closed?" Annie clutched the knob.

"Open," Jade replied while Jasmine said, "Closed."

"I'll leave it partially open."

Surprisingly, the two girls remained quiet, and Annie hurried toward Jeremy's room to see how the boy was doing. She rapped lightly on the door and waited for Ian to answer. A few seconds later, he appeared with a weary expression on his face.

He stepped into the hallway but glanced at Jeremy asleep on the bed. "I need to call a doctor I know who deals with seizures in children. I hope to get Jeremy in to see him tomorrow before his office opens. He'll need to run some tests and possibly prescribe medication for Jeremy. Will you watch him while I make that call?"

"Of course. I'll stay as long as you need me."

"Thanks. How are the girls?"

"They are in bed in Jade's room. They prayed and asked God to help Jeremy."

"Then, He's been bombarded with prayers this evening. I'll be back in a few minutes." Ian gave her a tired smile and headed for the staircase.

Annie checked to make sure Jeremy was still sleeping then took the chair Ian had been sitting in. She needed to come up with what she'd do when Jasmine was late to go to school. If not tomorrow, she would be probably soon, and the child needed to know the consequences. Annie could remember some of her own battles with her mother over boundaries and how neither parent ever backed down. No meant no. She realized she needed to talk with Ian to see how he'd want her to handle it.

Ian returned ten minutes later and motioned for her to join him in the hallway. Some of the tension in his expression relaxed as she came toward him.

"You couldn't have come at a better time. I don't know what I would have done if you weren't here. More and more I realize a person can't be in two places at once." One corner of his mouth hitched up. "Although I've been trying to these past months."

"Take it from me, it's scientifically impossible. I've tried myself, though. Did everything work out with the doctor?"

"Yes, Brandon will see him first thing tomorrow morning, but I'll need to postpone introducing you to the teachers until Tuesday. I've let the school know that you'll be bringing them and picking them up, so it'll be okay. The one thing that's working for us is they all go to the same school."

"So you want me to take Joshua, Jade and Jasmine in the morning?"

Ian nodded. "And be prepared for a hundred questions from Joshua the whole way. He'll want to know exactly what happened to Jeremy and what the doctor will say even before we know it."

"What do you think is happening?"

Sighing, Ian glanced toward his son in his room. "It could be epilepsy, but it takes more than one seizure to determine that." He rubbed his chin. "Now I'm wondering if some of Jeremy's behavior these past months might have indicated petit mal seizures. I haven't had a lot of experience with epilepsy, so I might be wrong."

"I'm glad I'm here for you and your family."

Ian grinned. "Just in the nick of time. Do you have any questions about tomorrow?"

"I may be wrong, but I have a feeling Jasmine will test me about getting ready for school on time."

"No, you aren't wrong. She even did with Aunt Louise. She has always been my prima donna, even as young as two. I think she was trying to be as different from Jade as she could."

"I've told her I won't allow her to make her siblings late for school, so I have a plan to stress my point." Annie looked into Ian's green eyes and for a second lost her train of thought.

"What?"

Okay, he had great eyes. She had to ignore them. Annie peered down the hall toward the girls' bedrooms. "She will ride with me to school dressed or not. I'll drop the others off, come home and let her finish getting ready, then take her back to school."

"But that's—"

"The consequence of having me drive twice to the school is that the next morning I will be waking her up thirty minutes earlier. That means she'll go to bed thirty minutes earlier, so she'll get the required amount of *beauty rest* she insists she needs."

Ian chuckled. "My daughter is an eight-year-old going on eighteen. I wish I had thought of that diabolical plan."

"So you're okay with it?"

"Yes. I like your creative way of dealing with it."

"I try to look for ways to have natural consequences for a child's actions. It tends to work better."

Ian checked his watch. "You'd better catch some sleep yourself."

"I'll peek in on the girls and Joshua, then leave."

She started to turn when Ian clasped her upper arm and stopped her. "Thanks again. Just taking the girls to their room and putting them in bed was a huge help."

Ian's touch on her skin riveted her attention

to his hand for a few seconds before he released his hold. Her heartbeat kicked up a notch. In her previous nanny positions she usually dealt with the mothers, but since Ian was a single parent she would be working with just him. She'd never thought that would be a problem—until now.

"It's part of my job," she murmured then continued toward Joshua's room next to Jeremy's.

When Annie climbed the stairs to her apartment, she stopped on the landing and rotated toward the yard. She saw a few lights off in the distance. The cool spring air with a hint of honeysuckle from the bushes below caressed her skin. The sky twinkled with stars—thousands scattered everywhere.

Her first unofficial evening had gone okay. It reinforced she'd made the right decision to work for Ian McGregor, instead of one of the other five offers she'd received. The family needed her, even more so because Ian was a single parent. Her only concern was the man she worked for: he was attractive, intelligent and caring, all traits she at one time had dreamed of in her future husband. Now, though, she thought of herself as a modern-day Mary Poppins, going where needed then moving on before her heart became too engaged. No sense getting attached.

* * *

Annie kept an eye on the kitchen clock while she scrambled the eggs, expecting the kids and Ian any second. When she glanced at the doorway, she spied Joshua dressed in the clothes they'd picked out together this morning. Other than his tennis shoes on the wrong feet, he appeared ready to go to school.

"Good morning, Joshua. Are you hungry?"

He nodded and plodded to the table, evidently not a morning person. He usually talked a lot, but earlier when she'd gotten him up, he'd said only a handful of words by the time she'd left him to dress.

As she turned off the burner, Ian and Jeremy entered the room. Neither looked happy. "Good morning, Jeremy, Ian." She set a platter of toast in the center of the table, then milk and orange juice. "Did you see Jade and Jasmine?"

Ian poured some coffee and settled into the chair at one end. "They were both supposed to be coming right away."

"I'm here," Jade announced from the entrance. She looked ready for school. "But Jasmine is still in the bathroom. She's decided to put her hair in a ponytail."

"I'll go help her." Annie placed the eggs next to the toast then started for the hallway.

"I tried. As usual, she didn't want my help." Jade plopped into the chair across from Jeremy.

Annie hurried up the stairs and poked her head into the doorway of the girls' bathroom.

Jasmine yanked the rubber band from her hair. "Ouch!" She stomped her foot and glared at herself in the mirror. "I can't do this."

"I can." Annie moved toward the child.

Jasmine whirled around, her lips pinched together. "No one can pull it as tight as I want."

"Okay. Breakfast is ready. We leave for school in half an hour."

"I can't be ready by then."

"That's your choice. You know what happens when you aren't ready." She'd informed Jasmine when the girls woke up. Annie left, preparing herself for the next hour and the battle to come.

When she returned to the kitchen, everyone watched her as she made her way to the table.

"Where's Jasmine?" Ian asked, finishing up his last bite of eggs.

"She doesn't need my help, so I reminded her of the time we're leaving for school." Annie sat at the other end of the table. "Which, Joshua and Jade, is in thirty minutes. Seven forty-five."

"I can't tell time," Joshua said as he stuffed a fourth of his toast into his mouth.

"I'll tell you. And you're ready except for brushing your teeth and changing your shoes."

"Why?"

"Dork, your shoes are on the wrong feet."

"Jeremy, that word is unacceptable." Ian carried his dishes to the sink.

"Well, he is one." Ian's eldest took his nearly full plate over to the counter then stormed from the kitchen.

"I'm not a dork. I like my shoes like this."

"It's not good for your feet. Here, I'll help you." Annie slid from her chair and knelt next to Joshua.

Once she fixed the problem, Joshua jumped up and raced toward the hallway. "I'm gonna be first ready."

"No, you're not." Jade quickly followed.

The sound of their pounding feet going up the stairs filled the house.

Ian came up behind Annie to help clear the dishes. "Ah, quiet. I've learned to cherish these moments. Is Jasmine going to be ready?"

"I don't know. She had her dress on but no shoes, not to mention she hasn't eaten breakfast."

"I'll be leaving right after you. I don't know how long we'll be at the doctor. He'll probably run some tests."

"How was Jeremy when he woke up this morning?" Annie hated seeing the concern and weariness on Ian's face. She hated seeing what Jeremy was going through.

"Grumpy, which isn't unusual, but when we talked about the seizure, I saw fear in his eyes. He rarely shows that. I tried to explain about what a seizure was, and he wouldn't listen."

"Denial. That's understandable. When Becca, my friend at school, had seizures she fought it. Finally she learned to accept the situation. Being less stressed helped Becca lessen the symptoms." Although she didn't have epilepsy, Annie had been in her share of denial while recovering from her third-degree burns. And she'd been angry at the world, too.

"Do you think Jeremy knew something was going on?" she asked. "My friend had petit mal seizures for a while before she had her first grand mal. I'd find her staring off into space, but she just said she was thinking."

Ian frowned. "It's possible. He's spent a lot of time in his room lately. I'd try talking with him, but he would just say his brother and sisters bothered him. I can remember going through a stage like that when I was a kid, so I thought it was that."

"It might be."

"It could explain some of what's been going on."

Annie caught sight of the clock. It wouldn't

do for the nanny to be late with the kids the first day on her job. Jasmine would never let her forget it if she didn't leave on time. "I've got to go. I might have to get up earlier tomorrow instead of Jasmine."

"I don't know if I'll be taking Jeremy to school today or not. It'll depend on what happens at the doctor. I'll keep you informed of what happens."

"Don't worry about the others. I'll take care of them." Annie went to the intercom and announced, "Time to go to school, everyone."

She heard a shriek from upstairs, then a few seconds later, Joshua and Jade hurrying down the steps, each trying to be the first out the kitchen door to the garage. If only she could get Jasmine to buy in to racing her siblings to the car.

With a deep sigh, Annie mounted the stairs. Jasmine came out into the hall carrying her shoes, her hair a wild mess as though she'd teased it. She'd changed her outfit.

"I need more time. I can't go to school wearing this. There's a stain on the blouse. I just saw it." The girl's voice rose to a shrill level.

"You have two minutes to make it down to the car in the garage."

Jasmine stomped her foot. "I have to look my best."

"Your choice. I can bring you back if you want to change, but I'm leaving in ninety seconds to take the other two. They have a right to be at school on time."

Jasmine charged into her room then returned with a blouse clutched in her other hand with her brush. "I hate you. You just don't understand." Tears filled her eyes as she marched past Annie, grumbling the whole way down the stairs, through the kitchen door and to the navy blue Ford Explorer. After Jasmine flounced into the backseat, she glared at Jade sitting in front.

Ian stood near the door from the breezeway, trying to suppress his grin. "I think I needed that. You know she won't get out of the car."

"I figured. Even if she changes her blouse and puts her shoes on, she would never go inside the school with her hair like that. I'll bring her home and let her get ready then take her back. She'll have to explain to the office why she was late."

"We'll need to compare our day this evening. I'm not sure whose day will be more challenging. Thank you again."

For a few seconds Annie felt as though they were in this together—but not just as employer and employee. With Ian's casual manner, it was easy to forget their relationship was strictly professional. "Nothing I haven't encountered before." Annie walked toward the vehicle, feeling Ian's gaze on her. It sent a shiver up her spine.

Later that night, after putting Joshua down, Annie went in search of Jasmine. Her door was closed while her twin's was wide-open with Jade sitting on the bed, listening to music. Annie rapped on Jasmine's door. Silence greeted her. She tried turning the knob, but it was locked.

She went to the entrance of Jade's bedroom. "Why is Jasmine's door locked?"

Jade waved toward her twin's room. "She told me she would go to sleep when *she* wanted."

Annie felt an urge to march down to Ian's home office and get a key from him to unlock the door right that minute. She curbed that reaction and instead said to Jade, "Thanks. She might go to bed when she wants, but she will be up earlier tomorrow."

"This is gonna be so much fun." Jade giggled and returned to listening to her music.

Annie neared Jasmine's room and said, "If you want your beauty sleep, you should go to bed soon. Good night."

Annie made her way downstairs to retrieve a key from Ian to have tomorrow morning. She knocked on his office door and he immediately said, "Come in."

Annie stuck her head into the room, expecting Ian to be at his desk trying to catch up on his work. But the chair was empty. She stepped farther in and spied him at the French doors to the patio, staring out at the night.

"I need a key to Jasmine's room. She's locked the door."

Ian turned, shaking his head. "How bad was it this morning?"

"She was an hour late because for forty-five minutes she refused to let me help her get the tangles out. When I took her to school, she said nothing the whole way. Tomorrow morning I'll wake her up early. If I have to, I have a bullhorn I can use."

Ian chuckled. "Thanks for the warning." He went to his desk and opened the top drawer. "I have a key that opens all their doors." When he pressed it into her palm, he added, "Keep it. It's a copy. This isn't the first time she's locked her door. It also comes in handy with Jeremy."

"How did it go with the doctor? Jeremy wouldn't talk about it. He just stalked off and slammed his bedroom door."

"He's not happy with what the doctor told him."

"Epilepsy?"

"There are a couple of more tests, but it looks like it, especially when Jeremy mentioned he's blanked out for a few seconds several times."

"Like what you told me when he got so angry at you in his room?"

Ian nodded, his forehead furrowing. "The doctor started him on antiseizure medicine today. I tried talking to him before bringing him home, but I got the silent treatment, too. I'm not sure what to do." He leaned back against his desk, gripping its edge.

"The only experience I have is with my friend, but there was a time Becca went through an angry stage. She was so scared she would have seizures at school. She didn't sleep at night, which wasn't good for a person with epilepsy." When Annie was eleven and this had happened to Becca, she'd been scared, too. She hadn't known what to do at Becca's first seizure. She'd hated feeling helpless.

"Yeah, I've been reading up on it. Stress and lack of sleep can lead to seizures. Did she get better?"

"Yes. When she did have a seizure at school, our teacher was great. Because she handled it matter-of-factly, the rest of us didn't flip out. She sent me to get the teacher next door and asked the class to step out in the hall. I got to stay because she knew we were friends."

Ian rubbed his chin. "I'm going to school tomorrow with you all, and I'll suggest that to Jeremy's teacher. If he knows there's a plan in place, it might help him feel better. They need to know what is going on, what's causing the seizures."

"My twin's husband, Ben, has a service dog. Ben came back from the war with post-traumatic stress disorder, although now he's doing much better. Ben's sister, Emma, trains service dogs. Emma's first husband had epilepsy, and she regretted that he didn't have the use of one."

"A service dog for epilepsy?"

"Yes, I wish my friend had had one in school. Emma is part owner of Caring Canines right outside Cimarron City. If you're interested, I could set up a meeting with her. That might be something that'll help Jeremy adjust better."

"We used to have a dog, but Aunt Louise was allergic to him so we had to give him away. A neighbor down the street took him. My children visit him from time to time and have asked me for another pet."

"A service dog is devoted to one person, although everyone will interact with him."

"So I should look into one for Jeremy and another dog for the rest of us?" Ian pushed himself away from the desk.

"It's a thought. But first you need to convince

Jeremy this will help him. We'll meet with Emma Tanner, the trainer, and she'll explain what the dog can do for him. Otherwise it won't work well if he doesn't agree to the dog."

"There's a lot to consider. There may be certain things my son will have to know and take into consideration, depending on how severe his epilepsy is, but I also want him to live as normal a life as possible. Jeremy was the most upset when we gave the dog away. In fact, for a long time he was angry at Aunt Louise, but she won him over."

"Then she died. That's a lot of loss to deal with, even for an adult."

A flash of pain darkened Ian's eyes. He frowned, plowing his hand through his hair. "I know. I think the only one not affected much was Joshua."

As Annie suspected, it was evident that Ian had his own battles with grief to fight. "Speaking of Joshua, has he always been adventurous?"

"From the second he could move around."

"On the way home from school today, he told me all about his day. I also got a little out of Jade but nothing from Jasmine. I know they can be difficult, but you have precious children."

Ian's eyes widened. "Where have you been all my life? I needed you six months ago. Of course, Tom would never have let me persuade you to come work for me instead."

The heat of a blush singed her cheeks. "There are other good nannies."

"Not from my perspective. So if you're planning to leave, please let me know. I'll offer you a deal you can't refuse. I never had this kind of conversation with the other nannies. Yes, with Aunt Louise, but not them."

Annie turned away, uncomfortable with compliments. The Hansens certainly had told her how important she was to the family, but for some reason it was different when Ian said it. She felt special and appreciated. "I'm going to check on the kids, then I need to get my own sleep. I'm getting up extra early so I can get Jasmine moving." Annie started for the hallway.

"Tomorrow, if Jasmine isn't ready, I could always carry her to the car then into the building."

At the entrance Annie turned around, not realizing Ian was only a few feet behind her. His nearness sent her heart beating faster. He was so close she caught a whiff of lime, most likely from his aftershave lotion.

Ian smiled, his eyes gleaming. "I'll check on Jeremy. I don't want him to run you off with the mood he's been in."

Out of all the children, Annie most identified with Jeremy because after the fire she'd felt what Ian's son was experiencing: angry at the world. "He won't run me off. It takes more than an angry kid to do that."

"Like what?"

Not feeling needed. But Annie wasn't going to tell Ian that. She shrugged. "Back to what you said about Jasmine—I considered that myself, but I'd rather the children decide to get in and out of the car. Taking a child kicking and screaming into a place will do more harm in the long run. At an earlier age, it might be the answer, but Jasmine is eight. Not only would it set her up for her classmates to make fun of her, it doesn't get to the root of the problem."

"That makes sense. Jasmine has always taken longer to get dressed than the others, but lately it has been worse. She won't even accept help. I remember she used to let Aunt Louise brush her hair. Now no one can touch it."

"Interesting. I wonder what made her change her mind."

"I'm not sure. Nothing she'll tell us."

"Maybe Jade knows. They may be very different in personality, but they're close."

"Yeah, they've always had a special bond. I should have thought about that." On the top step Ian angled toward her. "Why didn't I?"

"It's tough being a single parent with one or two, let alone four kids. Don't beat yourself up. Good night, Ian." Annie parted from Ian and made her way toward Jasmine's room.

Using the key, she unlocked the door and peeked in to see if she was in bed. She was, and Annie backed out. After checking on Jade, who was asleep, too, she walked to Joshua's room and slipped inside. She found him lying on the floor. Gently she scooped him up in her arms and placed him on his bed. When she began to straighten away from him, his eyes slid open halfway.

She brushed his hair away from his face and smiled at him. "You were on the floor with no covers." Then she kissed him on his forehead. "Good night."

"Annie, are you gonna leave us?"

"I don't have any plans to leave."

Joshua sighed and rolled over onto his side. "Good. All the others did."

As she backed out of the room, Annie's heart constricted at the need and longing in his voice. The best thing Ian could do to help his family was to find a wife. The kids needed a mother. As much as she could see that as a solution for him, she couldn't visualize him with a wife. The thought bothered her.

Chapter Five

The next morning, as Annie took the breakfast casserole out of the oven and placed it in the center of the table, Jade and Joshua came into the kitchen.

"It smells great. What is it?" Jade asked as she sat down.

"It's a recipe along the idea of French toast minus the syrup."

"Can I put syrup on it?" Joshua took his chair, staring at the dish.

"Try it first without. If you need syrup, then it's fine with me." When Joshua reached for the serving spoon, Annie added, "Wait until everyone shows up."

"Jasmine probably won't be down for a while. She's having trouble with her hair. I told her we need to shave it off, then she won't have any problem." Jade poured milk into her glass and Joshua's.

Joshua giggled. "That would be funny."

"No, it wouldn't be." Annie headed back to the counter. "Jade, could you help me put the rest on the table?" When she handed the girl the pitcher of orange juice, she said, "Jasmine used to let Aunt Louise help her with her hair. Do you know why she doesn't want help anymore?"

Jade nodded and took the drink. "The first nanny we had kept pulling her hair. When Jasmine screamed, she didn't care."

"Why didn't Jasmine say anything to your dad?"

"We just started pranking her. She didn't stay long."

"If you have a problem, you should tell your dad. I may have something to deal with the tangles." Annie followed Jade to the table and set down a tray of cut fruit.

When Ian came into the kitchen with Jeremy, Annie retrieved from a counter a spray bottle and brush she'd brought from her apartment and walked toward the door. "Start without me. I'm going to check on Jasmine."

"Jasmine's not ready. I told her we would be leaving in twenty minutes," Ian said.

"I know."

Annie found Jasmine in the bathroom, struggling again with her hair. "I got something for your hair. It was great for my sister. She had the same problem."

When Annie put the bottle on the counter, Jasmine scrunched up her face as if she wasn't sure about it.

"Try it and see. It works best when your hair is wet, but it still helps in dry hair to get the tangles out without a lot of pulling."

Jasmine tried brushing the back. She winced and cautiously reached for the bottle.

"Do you want me to spray the back and make sure it's all covered?"

The girl studied Annie in the mirror. "I guess, but I don't want you touching my hair."

"I won't unless you ask me, but it might make it better if I lift the hair and spray underneath, too. Okay?"

Jasmine clutched the brush but nodded warily, keeping her stare on Annie in the mirror. "It didn't used to be this bad."

"The longer it gets, the more tangles."

Jasmine's eyes grew round. "I love my long hair. No one is going to cut it."

With the patience she'd learned to cultivate as an aunt, Annie said, "I love your long hair, too."

"You do? Jade told me I should shave it off."

"She was kidding. Each person has to find what works for her. Shorter hair can be easier to manage, but as you see, my hair is long." She captured Jasmine's look in the mirror. "So here I go."

She sprayed the liquid on Jasmine's hair then took the detangling brush out of her pocket. "I got this, too, for you. Between the two you should be able to manage."

Jasmine looked stunned. "When did you get this?"

"This morning at the twenty-four-hour drug-store."

"For me?"

Annie smiled. "No sense pulling your hair out. If you need any help, I'll be downstairs eating breakfast. We leave in fifteen minutes."

The child stood still as Annie left. She hoped this helped Jasmine because she would have more important battles to fight with her.

When she reentered the kitchen, the kids and Ian were halfway through their breakfast. Ian saw her first. "How did it go?"

"We'll see." Annie sat, dished up part of the casserole then scanned the nearly empty plates at the table. "Do you want me to make this again sometime?"

All of them, even Jeremy, said yes.

"Great. It's easy because I make most of it the night before."

Jade finished first and hopped up.

"Jade, don't forget to take your plate to the sink." Annie ate a bite of the casserole.

"But I never—"

Ian scooted back his chair and picked up his dishes. "That's a good idea. Isn't it, kids?"

A few mumbles followed his question. Each one took his or her plate to the counter next to the sink and shuffled out of the room while Ian poured some more coffee.

"It was almost civil this morning except for a couple of outbursts from Jeremy."

"Is he concerned about going to school?"

"Hopefully when I talk to his teacher, he'll feel better."

"I hope so." Annie noticed Jasmine standing in the doorway, dressed, her hair pulled back in a ponytail. "You have a little time for something to eat." She remembered the child complaining all the way to school the second time yesterday that she was starving. "Five minutes."

Jasmine hurried to the table and looked at the casserole. "It's cold."

"There's fruit if you don't want to eat it cold. You should have been here on time, when the casserole was hot," Ian said.

While his daughter stared at the slices of fruit, Ian went to the intercom and announced they were leaving in four minutes. Suddenly she stuck a fork into a slice of pineapple and scooped up some grapes, then began stuffing them into her mouth. She never sat but started toward the hallway.

"Jasmine, please take your plate to the sink." Ian took a sip of his coffee.

"It's practically clean. All I put on it were some grapes."

"It will still need to be washed."

Jasmine snatched it up and rushed to the counter, then into the hallway to get her backpack and jacket.

"I haven't seen her move that fast in a long time. Did she let you do her hair?"

"No, but I gave her a couple of things to help with the tangles, and they obviously worked."

"Why didn't I think of that? Aunt Louise used to sit patiently and work her way through the tangles, but once, when she drove the kids to school, she got a ticket for speeding."

Annie chuckled. "They're girlie products—a detangler spray and brush. Most guys don't have hair long enough to tangle like hers."

"Jade's hair never tangles as bad as Jasmine's, but then Jasmine is a restless sleeper. I should take her to get it cut. Jade's been talking about cutting hers."

Typical of a man to think of the practical solution. "I wouldn't advise you to do that.

Jasmine loves her long hair. All she needs to do is learn to handle it."

"That's why it's good to have a woman around. My solution would have been taking her in for a cut."

"Kicking and screaming all the way." Annie chuckled.

Ian finished his coffee and set the mug on the counter. "Why can't she be more like Jade? Jade isn't nearly as dramatic as Jasmine. My biggest concern for her is getting a sports injury."

"I notice Jade's going to softball practice this afternoon." She pointed to the schedule she had put up on the kitchen wall. "You might take a look at that and make sure I've included all the activities."

As the four children poured into the kitchen, Ian said, "I'll take a look at it tonight and add anything of mine I need on it."

"Everyone ready?" Annie led the siblings to the garage.

Except for Joshua, everyone was silent on the trip to Will Rogers Elementary School. Ian took his own car.

After parking, Annie felt Ian's youngest clasp her hand and tug her toward the building. "I wanna show you my room."

Annie glanced back at Ian and the other three

walking behind her. What Joshua had said to her last night still touched her. And yet there would come a time when she would have to leave. She felt a heaviness in her chest.

After Annie met Joshua's teacher and saw where he sat in his room, the next stop was Jade's class then Jasmine's across the hall.

Jasmine's teacher smiled and said to her, "So glad you're here early today, Jasmine. But you don't have to come to the classroom until the last bell rings. I know some of your friends are in the hallway by the back door."

Jasmine put her backpack at her desk and hurried out of the room, passing Ian, Annie and Jeremy in the corridor making their way to his class.

Suddenly the boy stopped, looked away and said, "Dad, I don't want anyone to know about what happened. I'm taking the medicine. I won't have another one."

"Mrs. Haskell needs to know. We won't know about the medication's effectiveness until you've been on it awhile."

Jeremy's mouth dropped open. "You mean I could have a seizure at school?"

Ian nodded. "Not all your tests are back yet, and even then seizures can be unpredictable."

"Then, I don't want to go to school. Not until we know what's going on."

"You only have six more weeks, Jeremy. Nothing may happen during that time."

Fear washed over Jeremy's face. He backed away from Ian and Annie then whirled and raced down the hallway and out the door.

When Ian started forward, Annie touched his arm. "Let me see if I can find him. You need to talk to his teacher without Jeremy. He's scared." She knew that feeling well. Pain from her burns and fear of the unknown had flooded Annie when she woke up in the hospital after the fire. "I need to get some rapport with Jeremy. Let me try. We'll find you in a few minutes."

Later Annie found Jeremy in the parking lot by Ian's car. With his hands crossed over his chest, he slouched back against the Explorer. He saw her and turned away, but he didn't run.

Annie took that as a good sign. "I told your dad I would find you because he needs to talk with your teacher."

"Why? It's none of her business."

"Yes, it is. You're scared, but—"

He folded his arms over his chest. "No, I'm not. I just don't want other people knowing my business."

"I know how that feels."

"No, you don't. I saw a kid at school have a seizure once, and there were a couple of boys laughing."

"Did you laugh?"

Jeremy shoved off the car, his arms ramrod straight at his sides, his hands fisted. "I'd never do that. You don't know me."

"You're right. I don't, but I'd like to, Jeremy. I'm here to help you and your family."

"Yeah, until you find something better. Then you'll be gone just like that." Jeremy snapped his fingers in her face.

"I'm not leaving. I had five other job offers and chose to be with you all."

"Maybe you shouldn't have. I'd rather you leave now than later." Jeremy charged past her and hurried toward the building.

Annie followed, hoping he'd at least go to class. She was a little disappointed at how the conversation had turned out because she knew it wouldn't be easy for her to establish a connection with Jeremy. But she would keep trying. If Amanda hadn't with her after the fire, no telling where she would be today.

At the door into the school, Ian stopped Jeremy and talked quietly to him. Annie stood back, praying Jeremy would go into the building. She could remember how she had built up in her mind all kinds of scenarios if someone saw her scars. She could take a lot of different reactions, but pity was the worst.

When Jeremy stomped toward the entrance,

angry but going in the right direction, Ian signaled for her to join him. At Jeremy's classroom door, Ian paused for a few seconds, nodded his head then went inside.

"Mrs. Haskell, I wanted you to meet Annie Knight. She'll usually be dropping off and picking up my kids. I've given you her number in case you can't get hold of me."

Annie shook the middle-aged woman's hand. "I'm so happy to meet you. I want you to know I can be here in twenty minutes if there's a problem."

"I'm glad to meet you, too, Annie. I'll talk with Jeremy and reassure him," the woman whispered. "I've had other students with seizures, and I know what to do. We have a nurse who will be summoned. He'll be fine."

As Annie walked with Ian to the car, he said, "I guess all we can do is wait and see. I would like you to check into Caring Canines, if you don't mind, since you know one of the trainers." He paused at the trunk of the Explorer. "My family needs help."

"You've got it. I can set up a meeting with Emma Tanner."

"Let's keep it quiet. Until I know if this is going to be the best thing for Jeremy, I don't want to say anything to him. I'll have my receptionist call you with times I have available.

I do know that noon to one is usually free because my staff goes to lunch."

"I should know something tonight."

After Ian drove away from the school, Annie decided to pay Amanda a visit. She had met Emma at only a couple of combined family gatherings. Besides, she needed to talk to her sister.

A few days later, Ian shook Emma's hand. "I'm so glad you could meet with us."

Annie stepped forward. "It's nice seeing you again."

"Please have a seat." Emma indicated two chairs across from her in the training room. "Amanda told me you'd like to look into getting a seizure dog for your son."

"Since I asked Annie to contact you—" Ian glanced at Annie and smiled "—I've done some research on it. I want to give Jeremy everything that can help him. He isn't dealing well with the idea of having epilepsy."

"So he's been diagnosed?" Emma asked.

Besides Annie, whom he told on the way to Caring Canines, no one else knew, not even Jeremy, that the doctor had confirmed it this morning. "Yes. It appears he'd been experiencing a series of petit mals before he had his grand mal."

"What do you want from a seizure dog?"

To cure his son, but that wasn't a possibility. Seeing Jeremy even more vulnerable the other night when he'd had his seizure heightened Ian's own feelings of helplessness. "One that can alert people if Jeremy has a seizure, stay with him, help him adjust and be a companion, because right now Jeremy needs that. His life, especially in the past six months, has been disrupted again and again. He needs a dog to calm him down. Stress may have been a factor in what triggered his grand mal."

"I have a dog I'm training, but he needs a couple more weeks with me. I could use Jeremy helping me if you think he would like to do that. After school? What do you think?"

Ian grinned, excited at the prospect. "That would be great. Annie, will you be able to bring him here?"

"Sure. Emma, do you think the other three children could play with the other dogs? They're a four-year-old boy and twin girls who are eight."

"Sure. It would be nice if the dogs could interact with different people, especially children." Emma gestured around the large training room. "Our clients have doubled in the past few years. Abbey, my partner, and I are thrilled at all the interest."

"Then I'll be here with the kids, supervising," Annie offered.

"Madi, Abbey's sister-in-law, is often here with the dogs, as well. I'm teaching her to train. She's a natural."

Ian sat forward. "Do you ever have dogs you start to train but they don't work out?"

"Yes, but we also train therapy dogs and a lot of them can do that. A therapy dog is often used to help people through difficult or stressful times. Are you looking for another dog besides the service one?"

When Emma mentioned therapy dogs, Ian wondered if his family would benefit from an animal like that. "I've been thinking about getting a dog for my other three children. They've gone through two deaths in the family in the past two years. Would that interfere with Jeremy's seizure dog?" Ian hadn't thought about the two dogs clashing until now.

"Not necessarily, but if it's all right with you, I'd like to find a dog that's compatible with Rex, the black Lab I think might be a match for Jeremy."

"That's fine as long as it's good with children." Ian rose. "When do you want Jeremy to start?"

"Tomorrow is Saturday. Why don't you all

come out here and let Jeremy meet Rex, take a look around?" Emma got to her feet.

"I can come in the afternoon. I have several patients I need to see in the hospital in the morning."

"That's fine with me." Emma shifted toward Annie. "Every time I see you I think you're Amanda. I'm so glad you two wear your hair different or I might never tell you apart. Thanks for coming." Emma gave Annie a hug.

As Annie and Ian left Caring Canines, he glanced at her. "I need to meet this twin of yours. Does she work with children, too?"

Annie chuckled. "No, not yet. She wants to have children, but right now she works as an accountant. I'm glad someone in the family has a good sense of numbers. I struggled through algebra."

"Whereas my forte was math and science." Ian opened her car door for her.

"Well, I hope so since you went into medicine."

Ian rounded the hood and got in. Soon they pulled out onto the highway, heading into Cimarron City. "Since we live on the opposite side of town, you'll be driving a lot after school, especially when Jade goes to softball and Jasmine to ballet."

"I met Jasmine's teacher this week. A remarkable lady."

"Jasmine loves Miss Kit and ballet. They started rehearsing for their big end-of-the-year recital. That's all Jasmine talks about."

At a stop sign Ian peered at Annie. Being around the new nanny made him want to know all about her. He knew how she was with children, but she held part of herself back when they talked. Why? "What did you do as a child?"

"I was like Jade. Sports and camping. I was on the high school softball team until…" Her words faded into silence, and she averted her face.

"Did something happen?" Ian wanted to know what made Annie love children so much. She had a gift with them. In five days she had won over Jade and Joshua and was making progress with Jasmine. He hoped Jeremy would follow suit.

"I lost interest. That's all." Annie looked at him. "How about you?"

Ian glimpsed a flicker of sadness in her eyes, but it quickly disappeared. For some reason, he sensed it was more than losing interest that made her quit softball in high school. What? "After softball did you do something else?"

"No." Her tone was abrupt, tense. As if she was slamming a door in his face.

A car behind him honked. Forcing a chuckle to lighten the mood, Ian drove across the intersection. "I guess I should be paying more attention. I didn't know someone pulled up behind us. To answer your earlier question, I was a science geek and two years ahead of others my age. I went to college at sixteen, which I wouldn't recommend to others. I felt lost and socially behind, so I buried my head in my books."

"When did that change?"

"Who said it has changed?" Ian grinned.

"Ian, I've been around you for the past five days, and I haven't seen a lost and socially behind guy."

"Thank you. At least I think it was a compliment. Zoe, my wife, changed everything. She forced me to adapt because she loved the social life." He remembered their first meeting his senior year in high school. For the first year after her death, he couldn't even think about her without being swallowed in grief. Ian was thankful now he could think and talk about her without getting depressed.

"The kids don't say too much about their mom."

For months after Zoe died, Ian had spent much of his time in his home office working as if it would take his pain away. Aunt Louise finally had demanded he join the family more.

"That's probably because of me. I couldn't talk about her much at first. When they stopped asking questions, I was relieved."

"But those questions don't go away. They fester inside, waiting to be answered."

Ian clutched the steering wheel tighter. His defenses rose. "I haven't stopped them from asking." *Not in words anyway.*

"But have you encouraged them to talk about their mother?"

When Ian thought back over the past two years, he realized all he had done was survive from one day to the next. "No, but you think I should."

"My mother died when I was fifteen. For the longest time no one would say anything about her, especially me."

Had Annie's mother's death been what had stopped her from playing softball? Ian could sympathize with her about losing someone special and being thrown into a downward spiral. "I'm sorry about your mother."

Annie sighed. "Finally as a family we came together and talked about all the good memories we had of Mom. That helped me tremendously, but I didn't realize it until afterward. I went reluctantly to that family meeting."

Maybe I should start with a family meeting. "Annie, I need to eat lunch before going back to work. Do you want to join me, then I'll take you back to the house?"

"Sounds good."

"Good, because up ahead is one of my favorite restaurants." A few minutes later Ian pulled into the parking lot next to Doug's Steakhouse. "Give me a good juicy steak anytime."

"I'm not a big meat eater, but I'm sure they have a salad."

Inside, a waitress showed Ian and Annie to a table in the corner, not far from the stone fireplace.

After they ordered and received their iced teas, Ian said, "Tell me more about having a family meeting."

"It became a necessity for our family with seven children. We were often going in different directions, and besides breakfast in the morning, we didn't sit down together much."

"You got together for breakfast, not dinner?"

"We all started the day pretty much at the same time, but in the evening, some would be at practice or some other school activity, except Sunday-night dinner. Then we would eat together and have our family meeting. Nothing else could be planned during that time."

Would this help his children? Ian's focus had to be on healing his family. "What was your agenda?"

"Whatever we needed to cover, which varied, but there was a schedule of sorts. My dad would open with a prayer and my…mom would close with one." Annie dropped her gaze and cleared her throat. "After she…died, the eldest sibling took her place."

Ian could see her sadness, her struggle to continue, and he knew what she was going through. The pain of losing a loved one could surge to the foreground even after years. He reached across and covered Annie's hand, wishing he could do more to comfort her. "If you don't want to talk about—"

"No, I don't mind. I think a family meeting would be good for yours." Annie slipped her hands into her lap.

But she did mind—at least a part of her. It was written in her tension-filled expression. "What was the first order of business?"

"We each started out giving someone a compliment about something he or she did during the week. Usually it wasn't hard, except when my youngest brother went through his rebellious years. After that we dealt with the problems we were having. And not just those between the kids, but any we had with our parents, too. If something had to be decided, we came up with a solution as a group, but our parents could always veto it."

"Did they?"

"At the beginning when we made ridiculous decisions, but they always told us why. It didn't take us long to see the way we should go. We couldn't stay up till all hours of the night or skip our homework."

"How long did these meetings last with seven children?"

"Usually not too long—maybe an hour or two—unless one of us was straying and needed to be put on the right path. Those 'interventions' could last awhile." Annie picked up her tea and took a long swallow, her gaze on a spot to his left.

There was more to that, but Ian didn't feel he could ask about it. They were just getting to know each other, and Annie was good at putting up a wall. Had her family done an intervention with her? If so, why? In five days he felt she knew all about him and his family while he knew little about her, other than that she was excellent with children, caring and reliable. "After discussing the problems, what did you do?"

"We each told the group something good that happened to us during the week and what we were thankful for. Then the closing prayer."

The waitress brought their food. She set the steak in front of Ian and a Greek salad before Annie.

Ian cut his rib eye. "Okay, when you and your twin became the eldest, who said the closing prayer?"

She chuckled. "We traded each week, although technically Amanda was older by four minutes."

"A diplomatic way of handling it. I'm going to have to remember that with Jade and Jasmine."

"When do you think you'll start having the meeting?"

"I've got to do something. I should have months ago. You've seen us at meals. We don't really talk. Usually Jeremy is upset and angry at someone and everyone feels that tension."

Ian held his knife and fork poised over his steak. "It's been two years. I need to get my act together. I hope with your help."

Annie forked a few pieces of lettuce. "You have it."

A hint of red brushed her high cheekbones. There were times Annie acted shy, but other times she was a take-charge kind of person. She didn't like a lot of meat and usually ate little, but she loved bacon and had fixed it already several times, enjoying three or four pieces. She was a woman full of contradictions. A woman who fascinated him.

Ian drove the Ford Explorer on Saturday afternoon to Caring Canines with all the children packed into it. Annie looked back to see why everyone, even Joshua, was silent. He was nodding off while Jeremy, sitting next to him, was glaring at the back of his father's head. Jasmine was brushing her hair, and Jade's attention was glued to the ranch where the Caring Canines building was. Horses, some foals, frolicked in a pasture to the left while a lone one was on the right. Probably a stallion.

When Annie saw the training facility, she wondered if she'd had a therapy dog after the fire she would have recovered faster. At the beginning she wouldn't even talk to Amanda about her feelings concerning her mother and the guilt she felt. Instead, she'd kept it locked inside as though that would make it go away.

But it didn't.

Ian came to a stop in front. No one moved to get out of the car. He gripped the steering wheel so tight his knuckles whitened. Right before he'd come, Ian and Jeremy had had a huge shouting match with his son refusing to come. It was Joshua going into his big brother's room and calmly asking why he didn't want a dog that changed Jeremy's mind. Ten minutes later he agreed to go, but it was clear he wasn't sold on the idea of having a service dog.

Annie put a big smile on her face and turned toward the children. "Are you ready? When I was here yesterday they had twenty dogs being trained for various types of service. Do you know they have one for people with diabetes? It's amazing what these dogs can do."

Joshua grinned. "I wanna see. I want a dog, too."

"You can have mine," Jeremy mumbled under his breath.

"Oh, good." Joshua clapped his hands.

Ian finally twisted around and tried to smile. "I hope we can get two dogs. The one for Jeremy and another for the whole family."

"Let's go," Jade said, opening her door and hopping down.

Jasmine followed, although without much enthusiasm. Joshua waited, but when Jeremy wouldn't leave, the four-year-old scooted across the seat and exited with his sisters.

"I said I'd come to get Joshua to stop pestering me. I didn't say I would get out of the car." Jeremy crossed his arms and dropped his head.

Chapter Six

"I'll take the other kids inside," Annie said and shut her car door.

Ian looked pleadingly at Annie, not sure what to do. He remembered what she'd said about forcing a child to go kicking and screaming somewhere—it wouldn't work. *Lord, help me.* Annie smiled at him then hurried after the children.

Ian fortified himself with a deep breath then turned toward Jeremy. "We need to go inside, son. I've read about what a service dog can do for a person with epilepsy. It's there to help you through seizure and comfort you afterward. This could be good for you."

"How do you know it's good for me? You don't have epilepsy," Jeremy shouted as though he'd kept a plug on his feelings too long and they'd begun leaking out.

"True, but—"

"You don't know everything about me. I'm not sick. I don't need fixing. I don't need a babysitter or a dog." Jeremy hugged his arms against his chest as though he were freezing.

"I never said you were sick."

"I have to take medicine like a sick person."

"That's so you won't have a problem. It's for preventive reasons." Ian's stomach churned with frustration. Getting angry wouldn't solve this problem. "Go inside and at least meet Rex. Don't look at him as a service dog but as the one you wanted when we gave Lady away."

"I'm glad we couldn't get one. I don't want one now."

"Why? You love animals."

"I don't love anything."

Ian glimpsed the hurt behind Jeremy's declaration, and his heartbeat slowed to a throb. "You lost a lot in the past few years. We all have, but you can't give up on caring about others." As Ian said those words, he realized part of him didn't believe what he was saying. Wasn't that what he was doing? Shutting down his emotions and protecting himself from getting hurt again?

"You can't control how I feel."

"True. Tell you what. Meet Rex, and if you still don't want him after spending a few sessions with him, then we won't get him." Because no matter how much he wished it, Rex wouldn't work if Jeremy didn't buy in to the concept of a service dog.

"Sessions?"

"Mrs. Tanner wants you to help her with some of Rex's training. He has a couple of weeks before she feels he's ready to have an owner."

The tense set of his son's shoulders relaxed a little. "How many times do I have to see him?"

"Three. Today and two training sessions. Okay?" Ian prayed his son's love of animals—despite his denial—would have him saying yes to Rex.

Jeremy nodded and shoved open his door.

Before Ian could get out of his car, Jeremy charged toward the building entrance as though going into battle. Ian hurried to catch up.

Ian found his children with Annie and Emma in the fenced play yard out behind Caring Canines. Jeremy stood by the gate. "Let's go in."

"You didn't say I had to participate."

"But you do need to be with the dog. Whether you participate with Rex or not is your choice."

Ian opened the gate and let Jeremy go inside first.

"Jeremy, isn't Rex a beauty?" Jade petted the black Lab with golden-brown eyes.

"Yeah, he's so sweet." Jasmine held her hand out for the dog to lick it.

"Dad, I want this dog." Joshua sat on the grass while a puppy that was part terrier climbed all over him.

"We'll see, Joshua." Ian joined Annie and Emma near Rex while his eldest moved only a few feet forward.

When the twins turned their attention to a couple of the other dogs, Annie said, "It didn't go well?"

"I wasn't even sure if I would get him here." With Annie, Ian didn't feel as if he was alone fighting this battle with Jeremy.

"That's a shame. A service dog won't work for a person unless he wants him," Emma said, reinforcing what Ian already knew. She walked over to Rex, rubbed behind his ears and then headed toward Jeremy with the dog.

Ian tensed, not sure what his son would do. Jeremy straightened, his shoulders thrust back while Emma introduced Rex to him.

"If this doesn't work, I'm not sure what to do for Jeremy."

"Did he tell you why he didn't want Rex?" Annie faced him.

His gaze still trained on Jeremy, Ian said,

"He told me he wasn't sick, that he doesn't need fixing."

"It can be hard to accept something life changing like epilepsy, but a lot of children do get used to it. With some modification and the right medication, it can be manageable."

Ian glanced toward Annie, her nearness a balm. "Have you been reading up on it?"

"Yes. I like to be informed as much as possible, but I also know from experience with my friend."

Another thing Ian found he liked about Annie: she was proactive. "I realized in the car I couldn't make him take Rex. There are some things I can't resolve for him."

"Isn't that true with all your children?"

Ian faced Annie, her vanilla scent surrounding him. Everything about her, from her expressive face to even her fragrance, calmed him. "Yes. I'm finding that out. He's hurting, and I can't do a lot but be there for him."

"What did Jeremy say in the car?"

"He's lost too many people and a dog that he loved. He doesn't want to care about anything else." They were the same feelings Ian found himself fighting these days, so he knew exactly what his son was going through. "I think that's the biggest hurdle to having Rex. He was really beginning to respond to Aunt Louise when she died. Then we've had one nanny after another. I'm not sure he'll ever accept you, through no fault of yours."

"I'll keep trying. I'm not easily defeated when I set my mind to something."

The expression on Annie's face confirmed her words and reinforced yet again that Ian wasn't alone. For a long time he'd felt that way, even when Aunt Louise had come to help him. "I've seen that. I predict in a week or so that you and Jasmine will be best buddies."

"Well, I don't know about best buddies, but she'll accept help sometimes in order not to be awakened by my whistle. This morning she asked me for an alarm clock so she could get up by herself."

Ian chuckled. "That's not a bad idea for all the kids. We'll stop on the way home and let them pick out what they want."

"I predict Jasmine will want something pink and frilly."

"They make alarm clocks like that?"

With a grin, Annie nodded and turned to watch the children.

"Is she laying out her clothes the night before yet?"

"No, but she'll have to come to that conclusion on her own."

"I'm glad Joshua is, and he's taking your advice on what goes together."

Annie glanced over her shoulder at Ian. "Having his big sister laugh at his choice on Wednesday did the trick, and I didn't even ask Jasmine to do that. He assaulted her fashion sense with the purple-and-lime-green T-shirt and yellow shorts."

"It took all my restraint not to laugh out loud. He's always loved bright colors."

"Yes, I know. He's always coloring with bright crayons—and not necessarily on paper."

"Oh, look." Ian gestured toward Jeremy stepping closer to Rex and petting the top of his head. "I'd be encouraged if he wasn't frowning so much."

"Rex has two more visits to win him over." The pair started walking toward the kids.

When Ian had covered the distance between him and Jeremy, he knelt next to the black Lab and stroked him. "Rex reminds me of a dog I used to play with when I was young. He lived across the street and was so friendly. Does he do any tricks?"

"A few I taught him. Sit. Lie down. Stay. Come. Lose it." Emma turned to Jeremy. "Here, I'll show you some of them."

Good thing Emma didn't ask his son if he wanted to see the tricks. Judging from his sour

expression, Ian expected Jeremy would have probably said no.

After Rex demonstrated sit, lie down and come, Emma withdrew from her big apron pocket a treat. "Stay, Rex." Then she went a few feet away and put the bone on the ground. Rex fixed his attention on the treat but didn't move. "Come." He rushed the bone and snatched it up. "Lose it." Rex dropped it.

Jeremy watched with a gleam of interest in his eyes but didn't say anything.

"Now, I'd call that a well-trained dog. What do you think, Jeremy?" Ian asked, encouraged by the boy's attention to Rex.

His son lifted his shoulders, spun around and headed for the gate.

After Emma gave Rex the treat, she straightened and said quietly, "He hasn't accepted his situation yet."

"No, but he promised me he would come for two training sessions with Rex. I'm hoping that will change his mind."

"I'll do my best to draw Jeremy in."

"Thank you, Emma." Ian pointed to his other kids. "As you can see, the rest would love to have a dog."

Over the sounds of Joshua giggling as the puppy licked his face, Annie joined Ian, looking

around. "This may not have been a good idea. Each one has gravitated to a different dog."

Ian said, "Jasmine, Jade and Joshua, it's time to leave. You all will be coming back on Monday."

Jasmine said goodbye to a black poodle while Jade hugged a cocker spaniel. Joshua ignored his dad's announcement.

Annie smiled. "I'll take the girls and find Jeremy. We'll be at the car. Have fun trying to get Joshua to come with you."

"I'll trade jobs," Ian said then walked toward his youngest, the sound of his laughter sweet to hear. For a brief wild moment, he considered getting a dog for each of them but quickly dismissed it. Annie would be stuck with caring for all of them, and he didn't want to lose her.

Ian sat on the grass next to Joshua. "He's cute."

"I wanna take him home. Can I?"

"No, he isn't ours to take. He belongs here, but you're coming back on Monday."

Joshua picked up the squirming puppy and held him against his chest. "I don't wanna leave." His lower lip stuck out. "I wanna stay."

Ian had one son who couldn't get out of the place fast enough, and the other he would have to pry away from the puppy. Ian took the terrier mix and passed him to Emma standing nearby. "We've got to go. If you don't leave now, Joshua, you won't get to come back on Monday." Which meant he would have to find someone to watch him, since Annie would be with the other children. When Joshua jumped up and ran for the gate, relief washed over Ian, and he hurried after his son to make sure he didn't let the dogs out.

As they strolled toward the building, Joshua took Ian's hand. Something as simple as that reminded him how much he loved each of his children.

At the car Joshua climbed into his car seat, and Jade buckled him in. In the far back sat Jasmine, while Annie slid out of the Ford Explorer and motioned to Ian to come near.

When he did, she whispered, "I think Jeremy was having a petit mal seizure when we were getting into the car. For a few seconds, he didn't respond or even know we were here."

"Thanks. I wonder how many he has that we never see."

"It's hard to say. I'm trying to keep an eye on him, but he loves to stay in his room."

Before Annie got back into the front seat, Ian clasped her hand. "Thanks. With everything that has been happening, I'm feeling a tad bit overwhelmed."

One of her eyebrows arched. "Only a tad?"

"I was trying to be tough and strong and not admit the full extent." Ian smiled and rounded the hood of the SUV, wondering what he would be doing without Annie's help.

On Sunday evening Annie sat on one side of Joshua while Ian was on the other. The rest of the children were seated in chairs in the den so that the family formed a loose circle.

Ian finished the opening prayer, took a deep breath and said, "This is our first family meeting, but we are going to have one every Sunday evening at this time."

"Why? What's a family meeting?" Jasmine asked.

"It's a time we hash out any problems we're having. But not just that. It's also when we can talk about the good things happening to us." Ian shot a look at Annie, as if to tell her to step in at any time.

Annie held up a squishy yellow ball. "Only one person should talk at a time so we can hear what's being said. The person with the ball will have the floor but can't hold it the whole time." She passed it to Ian.

"I thought we would start by telling the person to our right one thing good about them. I'll start." He turned to Joshua, saying, "You were ready for school every day this week."

Then he gave his youngest the ball and pointed to Annie.

"I love your pancakes. Can we have them again?" Joshua grinned and passed the ball to Annie.

Looking at Jasmine, Annie tried to decide what to say. "Jasmine, I think your idea about an alarm clock was great."

By the time it was Jeremy's turn at the end, his frown had evolved into a scowl. "This is a dumb idea." He tossed the ball to his dad.

"I need to go over the few rules we'll have. If you can't tell someone something good, don't say anything. When you're through talking, put the ball on the coffee table. Then the person who wants to talk will grab it. If we are discussing a problem, everyone needs to listen to the others. Every family member has a voice in this meeting."

Joshua snatched the ball from his dad's hand. "Even me?"

Ian laughed. "Yes. During the week if you have a problem you want to talk about, write it down on the chart in the kitchen. Joshua, you can have Annie or me do it for you. Some things have to be dealt with immediately, but there are a lot that we'll be able to decide as a family. Oh, and the last rule is no shouting.

Speak in a calm voice." Ian put the ball on the table.

Annie knew that would be the hardest one to keep for some of them.

Jade took the ball and said, "I like this, and I have a problem I want to talk about. We need a dog."

Through the discussion about having a dog everyone gave an opinion except Jeremy. He folded his arms over his chest and lowered his head.

"It looks as though you all want to get a dog. We saw some yesterday. Which one do you think would be best?" Ian looked around the circle while Jasmine, Jade and Joshua gave their suggestions.

Suddenly Jeremy shot to his feet. "I don't want a dog! I don't need Rex!" Then he whirled around and ran from the room.

Annie remembered the time she'd hurried away when her family gathered to talk to her about the fire. No matter how much they reassured her, the guilt still ate at her. If only she'd blown out the candle before going to bed, her mother would be alive today. That fact wasn't going to change. But slowly the anger toward others had abated, and she'd learned to deal with her anguish internally rather than lash out at her family.

Annie stood. "I'll check on Jeremy while you guys talk." She wanted somehow to get through to the hurting child. She knew what deep pain Jeremy was in.

Ian nodded.

Annie headed for the staircase to check Jeremy's room, where he usually hid out. But when she started down the hallway, she noticed the door was open, and he kept it closed when he was there. After checking it and the bathroom the children used, she went through the rest of the house then returned to the den and motioned for Ian.

He came out in the corridor. "What's wrong?"

"Jeremy isn't inside. I wanted you to know before I look outside. Does he have a special place he would go?"

"No. I'll take the back while you search the front." He poked his head into the den. "Jasmine and Jade, watch Joshua. We'll be outside."

While Ian made his way to the kitchen to go out to the backyard, Annie stepped out onto the front porch. About forty-five minutes of daylight were left. She prayed they found him before that.

Descending the stairs to the sidewalk, Annie looked up and down the street and spotted Jeremy three houses away, sitting on the curb.

She started to yell his name but didn't, afraid

Jeremy would run. Instead, she went to the gate on the side of the McGregor home and quickly found Ian in the backyard. “He’s a few houses away.”

Ian joined her, and they started for Jeremy, who was still sitting at the curb. The boy looked up and spied them coming. He bolted to his feet and turned to flee. He took two steps and then collapsed to the ground, his body stiffening and quaking.

Chapter Seven

"Keep track of the time," Ian shouted as he hastened to his son. His heart pounded his chest the way his steps pounded the earth as he cut the distance to Jeremy. "Son, I'm here. You'll be all right," he said in as soothing a voice as possible. He didn't know if Jeremy heard him or not, but he wanted him to know he wasn't alone.

Wishing he had something to cushion Jeremy's head, Ian turned him on his side and protected his thrashing body as much as he could without restraining him.

When Annie arrived, he glanced at her. "How long?"

"One minute but he's calming down some." Annie gestured toward Jeremy on the small patch of grass between the street and sidewalk. "Thank God he hit the ground, not the concrete."

Ian closed his eyes for a second and sent up a prayer. Finally—an eternity in Ian's mind—Jeremy's eyelids stopped fluttering, and his rigid body began to relax. Ian checked his son for any injuries caused by the fall.

Behind Annie, a neighbor asked, "Is there anything I can do to help?"

Ian glanced up and noticed several others who lived on the street standing around. "He'll be okay. Thanks for your concern." Then to Annie, Ian added, "I'm going to carry him back to the house."

She nodded and asked the people to move back.

Ian wanted to get Jeremy inside before he became angry, his probable reaction when he came out of the seizure, especially if he saw all the people watching him. Although not unconscious, Jeremy hadn't gotten his bearings yet, his gaze still dazed.

Annie went ahead of Ian and opened the front door, only to find all the children gathered in the foyer.

"Is Jeremy okay?" Jade chewed her bottom lip.

"Did he have a seizure?" Jasmine rubbed her hands up and down her arms.

Joshua's eyes filled with tears.

Ian answered, "He had a seizure, but he'll

be fine. Go with Annie and start getting ready for bed."

"But it's too early—"

"Jasmine, go." Ian started for the staircase while Annie tried to calm them.

He'd seen people have seizures before, but when it was his son, he needed to detach himself to handle it in a matter-of-fact way. Otherwise his children would sense all the emotions rampaging through him. With time he prayed he'd do a better job of masking his fear that Jeremy wouldn't pull out, and he'd lose him like Zoe and Aunt Louise.

When Ian placed Jeremy on his bed, he caught his son's look, his forehead knitted.

"What happened?" Jeremy murmured, blinking his eyes several times.

"You had a seizure in front of the Clearys' house."

Red flooded Jeremy's pasty complexion. "Who saw me?"

"A few of our neighbors. All adults."

Jeremy firmed his mouth in a hard line and rolled to his side. "I'm tired."

Ian backed away from the bed. He removed a pile of clothing on a chair then sank down onto it. He didn't feel comfortable leaving Jeremy. What if he had another seizure on top of this one? More than ever he realized Jeremy needed a dog to let Ian or Annie know when he had a seizure. What happened outside earlier could have ended badly, and Ian might not have known about it. He didn't want to restrict his son's activities, but he might have to until his medication controlled his seizures better. Ian didn't look forward to yet another battle with Jeremy, but his safety came first.

A sound behind him drew his attention. Annie started toward him, but he rose, palm out, and made his way to her, moving out into the hallway. He didn't want Jeremy overhearing any discussion about him.

"How is he?" Annie asked, her large brown eyes full of concern. "The kids have a million questions. I told them I'd talk to you. They're worried."

"He's alert now. He told me he's tired, but that may also be his way of avoiding talking to me."

"If you want, I'll sit with him while you talk with the kids."

"Thanks. I need to reassure them." And hope he could put at least their fears to rest. "I want to call his doctor, too. Good thing Brandon's a friend."

"Don't worry. I'll take care of Jeremy while you do that, and if you need me to stay part of the night with him while you sleep, I can."

For one impulsive moment, all Ian wanted to do was hold Annie in his arms and draw comfort from her. When he'd first met her, he'd thought she wasn't ugly but not a beauty, either. But now all he saw was a woman whose beauty shone from deep inside her. Would things have been different with his children if she'd been their first nanny rather than the fourth one? Would Jeremy have come to him about his concerns about blanking out?

"I'm going to sleep again in his room. It worked okay the other night, but I appreciate the offer. You come back here from your day off and end up dealing with all this."

"When children are involved, schedules and plans often get discarded. I'm used to it." She smiled.

He chuckled. "I'll be back in a little while. Kids first, then Brandon."

Ian found the children in Jade's bedroom, his two daughters sitting on the bed with Joshua between them. He'd been crying, his eyes red. The twins were comforting him. Now Ian had to do the same for all three of them.

He lifted his son into his arms. "Your big brother will be okay."

"He isn't gonna die?"

"No, he'll be fine." Jeremy's health wasn't in his control, but it felt right saying that to his children. Ian sat at the desk and placed Joshua on his lap. "Annie said you all are worried and have questions. I'll try to answer them."

"Is this gonna happen all the time?" Jade scooted back on her bed and crossed her legs.

"I don't know. I hope not. I hope the right medication dosage can be found soon to control the seizures."

"I saw him on the ground. Did he fall?" Jasmine asked.

"Yes, sometimes a person's muscles go slack and he drops. So you were looking out the window?"

Jasmine nodded.

"How much did you see?"

"Not much. You blocked my view. What do we do if one of us is the only person around?"

"Good question, Jasmine. Get help. Place something soft under his head. And if you can, roll him onto his side, but don't hold him down. Sometimes a person who has a seizure flails and thrashes. He could hurt you and himself if you try stopping him. You should move anything dangerous away from him. Above all else, be calm and stay close until help comes. The seizure will run its course." As he said this, his children's eyes grew rounder, and none of them spoke.

"Calm? How?" Jade finally asked.

"I know the first time I saw a seizure, it scared me, but remember Jeremy will get better. Talk to him if you want. Tell him he'll be okay." If they said it, hopefully they would believe it. It had helped Ian to do that.

"I'm scared." Joshua snuggled against Ian.

"I know it can be scary, but don't let Jeremy know that. He already feels as if people think he's strange. Come to me instead. Everyone has problems. Joshua, you do something without thinking about if it's dangerous or not. Jeremy has seizures. That's his problem right now."

Jasmine glared at Joshua. "Yeah, remember when you were standing on the railing? You could have really hurt yourself. You scared me."

"And me," Ian added.

"It wasn't gonna hurt me. I wasn't scared. I had my cape on."

Jasmine leaped to her feet, her arms straight at her side. "You can't fly with a cape." With a huff she said, "I'm going to lay out my clothes for tomorrow and get ready for bed." She marched from the room.

"Did I hear right? She's choosing what she's gonna wear now?" Jade shook her head in wonderment.

"Yep." Ian stood, holding Joshua in his arms. "And it's time for you to get your pj's on and brush your teeth."

"I don't wanna go to bed."

"Sorry, dude. You have school tomorrow." He carried his youngest from Jade's room, set him down and watched as he scurried to his room.

Ian walked toward his bedroom to call the doctor and passed Jeremy's. He glanced in the doorway and spied Annie. Of late, he'd felt as if he was taking one blow after another. If it hadn't been for Annie this past week, he didn't know if he could have kept it together. But he had—because of her presence.

Tuesday all the children piled out of the Ford Explorer and hurried to Caring Canines. Jeremy remained in the front seat, staring out the windshield.

"You worked well with Rex yesterday." Annie removed the key from the ignition.

He harrumphed.

"You didn't say much when I picked you up from school. Everything go okay today?"

"It was just great," he said in a sarcastic tone.

"What happened?"

"Nothing."

"Sometimes talking about it helps."

Jeremy swiveled around and narrowed his eyes. *"Nothing happened."* He drew those two words out.

"Okay, that's great." Annie heard the doubt in her voice. She was sure Jeremy knew she didn't believe him.

He pressed his lips together, his gaze scissoring through her. "Okay. I was moved to the front of the classroom this morning, close to the teacher's desk like I'm a troublemaker. I haven't done anything wrong."

"Did you talk to your teacher about it?"

"Yeah. She wanted to keep a closer eye on me. Even Joshua, Jasmine and Jade look at me like I'm weird."

"How so?"

"As if they're waiting for me to have a seizure and worrying what they're gonna do."

"The unknown is scary for them and they love you, so they're worried."

He crossed his arms. "I'm not broken."

"I know that. You know it and your dad does. It might take others a little more time."

Jeremy shoved open the door, stepped out and walked toward the building.

As Annie followed, her cell phone rang, and she saw it was Ian. She greeted him then said, "We just arrived at Caring Canines."

"Good. My last patient canceled, so I'm heading there. Did Jeremy give you any problems?"

"Nope. He's already inside." Annie opened

the door and slipped into the building, the sound of dogs barking in the background.

"His teacher called and said Jeremy was angry when he left. He got moved to the front by her desk, and he doesn't want to be there. He doesn't want any special treatment. I'll email her and see if she'll move him back."

"I'm not sure you should. That might draw even more attention to him."

"True. I'll see what happens this week. I'm turning into the ranch. I'll be there in a moment."

Annie said, "See you soon." She disconnected and returned her cell phone to her pocket then continued her trek to the back training room to make sure Jeremy was working with Emma and Rex. She paused at the doorway.

For all his complaining about attending, Jeremy was focusing his attention on what Emma was saying, Rex sitting next to him. Suddenly Rex got up and went behind Jeremy just as the boy crumbled to the floor, keeping his head from hitting the tiles.

Emma rolled him on his side and glanced at her watch while Annie found a small pillow and placed it under his head. Rex positioned himself next to Jeremy.

"I think Rex sensed the seizure coming on." Emma looked up at Annie. "I didn't see anything until he started dropping to the floor, but Rex was behind him before he fell."

"They're connecting." Annie heard the sound of footsteps in the hallway. "Ian is coming."

As Ian entered the room, Jeremy came out of his seizure, confused, scowling. Rex wiggled closer to Jeremy and settled down.

"How long was this one?"

"Ninety seconds," Emma replied and moved so Ian could check his son. "Rex cushioned Jeremy's head, so he didn't hit it on the floor when he went down."

"Is Rex okay?" Ian stroked the dog next to his son.

Emma ran her hands over the black Lab. "He's fine. That's one of the ways a service dog is able to help."

Annie remembered the other children outside and said, "I'm going to check on Jasmine, Jade and Joshua."

As she made her way to the outside play area, she hoped Madi was out there today like yesterday. The twins had listened to every word the teenage girl said. Jade had even declared on the way home that she wanted to volunteer at Caring Canines like the owner's sister-in-law.

Outside, Madi leaned against the chain-link fence talking to Jade while Joshua played with the cocker spaniel Jade had on Saturday. Annie opened the gate and walked into the enclosure as Jasmine turned her attention to the cocker spaniel.

"What's her name?" Jasmine called out to Madi.

"Daisy. She's a sweetheart. I wish I could have another dog, but my brother says I already have a kennel full."

Jade smiled at Annie then turned to Madi. "Is she going to be trained?"

"Maybe as a therapy dog. She was left a few weeks ago out by the gate."

"I can't believe people dump their pets like that." Jade knelt near the cocker spaniel.

"It happens at least once a month. It makes Abbey and Emma mad. I help them find homes for the ones that aren't trained. Have you all decided on a dog to take home yet?"

"We can pick today?" Joshua asked.

Madi looked at Annie who answered, "Yes, if you three can decide on one. Your dad talked with Emma yesterday about it." Then in a lowered voice, Annie continued, "Madi, I need to go inside to see how Jeremy is doing. Will you help the children choose a dog?"

Madi grinned. "I would love to."

At the door into the building, Annie glanced over her shoulder at the three children with Madi sitting on the ground in a circle around

Daisy. Knowing they were in good hands, she hurried inside to see what was happening with Jeremy. As she approached the training room, Jeremy ran out, anger stamped on his face.

She started to go after him but stopped to see what Ian wanted her to do. She stepped into the room. His haggard look showed how bad the situation must have gotten. "Do you want me to try talking to him?"

"You can try. He wouldn't listen to Emma or me. I'll go get the other children. We need to leave and let Emma get back to work." Defeat coated each word.

Annie wanted to comfort him, but at the moment Jeremy was her priority. The torment the child was going through tore at her heart. Annie found him on the other side of the Ford Explorer, sitting on the pavement, crying.

Suddenly a memory intruded into her thoughts: the first day she'd glimpsed herself in a mirror after she'd been discharged from the hospital. Stunned and broken, she'd sunk to the floor and sobbed at the sight of the red scars from what remained of her right ear and across her torso to her left hip, where the beam had landed on her.

No one could reach her at that time. She wouldn't listen. But she had to try with Jeremy.

She didn't want him to go through the heartache she did.

She sat next to the child, about a foot away, and rested her arms on her raised knees. Staring off at a pasture with a stallion, she remained silent, waiting for Jeremy to say something. He needed to let his emotions out, then she would see if she could help.

Slowly his tears abated and he peered at her, more drained than angry. "Why are you here?"

"To be here for you."

"I don't need..." Tears welled into his eyes again, and he knuckled them away.

"Everyone needs someone, Jeremy. What you're going through isn't easy. I know. I went through something similar when I was fifteen."

"You had seizures?"

"No, something different, but it affected my whole life."

Jeremy's forehead wrinkled. "Then, you don't—"

Annie turned toward him and lifted her hair away from the scarred side of her face. "I was in a fire and burned badly from here—" she ran her hand across her chest to her thigh "—to here and was in the burn unit for weeks. I went through several operations. I missed a semester of school."

Jeremy's eyes widened while she combed her hair back into place.

"It changed my life. My mother died in that fire, and I miss her every day."

His bottom lip trembled.

"I don't tell people about it. I still try to hide it, and I prefer that you don't say anything until I at least tell your father and your siblings myself. My burns could define who I am if I let them. You can let your seizures define you if you want, but they aren't really you."

Jeremy blinked, opened his mouth to say something but snapped it closed.

"I worried about people staring at me, making fun of me or looking at me horrified. The people I loved never did, and I learned over time the others weren't important. The first person outside my family to visit me was my friend Becca, who had epilepsy. She accepted me for who I was and was there to support me. I was so angry I didn't make it easy for her to stick by me."

Jeremy looked at the stallion. "I don't want to die from a seizure."

"Why do you think you will?"

"My mom had one in the hospital right before she died."

"I understand from your father your mother

died from a stroke. That can sometimes cause a seizure, but you aren't having a stroke."

"Then, why am I having seizures? What did I do wrong?" A tear ran down his face, and he swiped it away.

"Not a thing, Jeremy. Things happen to us that we have no control over. That's when we have to turn our lives over to the Lord and not worry about the future. It's in His hands. About the only thing worrying does is stress us out, and that's not healthy. Jeremy, have you told your dad about your fears and your mother?"

Jeremy shook his head. "Mom's death makes him sad."

"He'd want to know this. You should talk to him." Annie knew how much Ian loved his children. He made mistakes like all parents, but he was a good father.

"Maybe." He looked again at the stallion.

"May I tell him? I won't if you don't want me to."

A long moment passed before Jeremy finally nodded.

"How about Rex? I saw him cushion your fall. Rex can do some amazing things."

"I know, but I don't want to take him to school. The kids will know something is wrong with me."

"Why don't you tell them? Most kids would

be interested, especially your friends. And dogs are a great way to start a conversation."

"Maybe."

"Your dad is rounding up the other children to leave. If you think you might take Rex, you need to let him and Emma know."

"Rex was right next to me. He even licked my face."

"You'll never be alone when you have a seizure with Rex."

"He'll sleep with me?"

"Yes. He'll become your buddy. I understand you used to have a dog and loved her."

"Yeah. She died. I don't want to lose another pet."

Annie heard Joshua's voice, which meant the family was almost at the cars. "Death is hard, but it's part of life. If you never have a pet, you can't enjoy years of companionship with one." She rose and held out her hand to help Jeremy to his feet.

He stared at it a few seconds then clasped it. "I won't say anything to the others about your scars." His words, spoken in a serious tone, forged a bond between them.

"Thank you."

When Jeremy stood, his siblings climbed in the other side of the Ford Explorer while Ian talked with Emma at the entrance into the building. He held a leash with the cocker spaniel on it.

"It looks as though your brother and sisters picked Daisy as their pet."

Jeremy skirted the front of the Ford Explorer and walked toward his father.

Annie trailed Jeremy to find out what was going on concerning Rex.

Daisy greeted Jeremy with her tail wagging. He patted her, then stood next to his dad.

"Have you decided to continue training with Rex?" Ian asked.

"Yes, but I don't know about taking him to school."

Ian clasped his son's shoulder. "We'll take it one day at a time."

"You won't make me?"

"No. I think you'll find Rex is good for you and want to take him." Ian turned to Emma. "I guess they'll be back tomorrow. Okay?"

"Yes. Jeremy, Rex is already bonding with you so I'm glad you decided to continue the training."

Ian said, "For the rest of this week, I'll clear my schedule so I can bring Jeremy. I want to be involved." He shook Emma's hand.

As Jeremy, Ian and Annie walked toward the Ford Explorer, the boy said, "You don't have to if you don't want to, Dad. I'll be okay."

"I know that, son, but I saw Rex in action today, and it's fascinating to see what a dog can do to help people."

"In the meantime, your sisters and brother can acclimate Daisy to your home so hopefully they won't complain too much that they aren't coming." Annie opened the back door to the Ford Explorer and the cocker spaniel got in with Jade's assistance.

While Jeremy slid into the front seat, Annie accompanied Ian toward the rear. She paused and lowered her voice, saying, "Jeremy said I could tell you. One of his concerns is that his mom died after a seizure."

Ian closed his eyes for a few seconds. "I forgot he was visiting his mom when she had her last stroke, and she did have a seizure. Everything got so hectic after that. I wish he'd said something to me."

"He thought you were sad when you talked about your wife."

Ian sucked in a large breath and released it slowly. "He's right. I'll have a talk with him. In fact, I will with each of my children. They need to know they can come to me with anything."

"Sounds good. See you at home." Annie turned toward the SUV.

Ian caught her arm. She glanced back at him. The look of appreciation in his eyes made her feel special in that moment, more than she had in a long time.

"Annie, I don't even know where to begin thanking you for your help."

She covered his hand with hers, the physical connection making everything, except the man near her, fade from her consciousness. She smiled. "You just did." Then she continued around the Ford Explorer to the driver's side, missing his touch. Too dangerous for her to get used to that. Annie had let down her defenses in college, risked her heart with David and ended up brokenhearted. She couldn't go through that again.

Annie realized as she started the car that when she'd said, "See you at home," she'd felt as if Ian's house really was her home. More than she had at any place she'd worked as a nanny. The realization stunned her.

Later that night Annie fixed herself a cup of tea to sip while she read a suspense story. After the eventful day, she needed some downtime before trying to sleep. Dinner earlier was the first time that Jeremy hadn't been angry or ready to argue over everything being discussed. He even paid attention to Daisy. The dog chose to sleep with Jade, much to Joshua's disappointment.

As Annie moved toward the living area in her apartment with her drink, a knock sounded at the door. She detoured and opened it to find Ian standing on the landing. "Is Jeremy okay?"

"Yes. They all are, even Jade with Daisy. I won't keep you, but I wanted to thank you again for letting me know what was going on with Jeremy. Tonight he actually participated in the dinner discussion. I wish he'd felt he could tell me, but at least he told you. I intend to talk to him tomorrow on the way home from Caring Canines."

"You're welcome, Ian. Come in. I need to talk to you."

"As long as you don't give your notice." He grinned.

"No, definitely not that, but it's something I should have told you from the beginning."

Confusion clouded his face as he shut the door and moved toward the living area, sitting down on a chair while she took the couch.

"Sorry. That sounds as though it's serious. Well, I guess it is but only to me." Ian's intense look, as though he were trying to figure out what she was going to say, made her nervous. "Something wrong?"

"No." Annie swallowed hard. "I told Jeremy about a problem I had as a teenager and how hard it had been on me. I was angry at life. I feel I need to tell you, too, and if it's okay, I want the rest of your children to know."

"What are you talking about?"

Annie glanced toward the kitchen, stalling. "Would you like some tea?"

Ian sat forward in his chair kitty-corner from her on the couch and took her hand. "No, but I would like you to tell me before I go crazy wondering what you want to say."

Her breath trapped in her lungs, Annie brushed back her hair and pushed her turtleneck collar down to reveal her scarred ear and neck.

Chapter Eight

Deeply scarred tissue, mostly red with a few white streaks, took Ian by surprise. He'd been thinking all kinds of things Annie could tell him, but this wasn't one of them. "What happened?"

"I was in a fire at our family cabin. A beam fell across me, pinning me. My father managed to rescue me, but not—my mother in the other room." Tears filled her eyes.

The urge to comfort her overwhelmed him. Ian had helped burn victims throughout his career, and the pain associated with that kind of injury was intense. He moved to the couch, drawing her against him. If in that moment he could have wiped the memory and effects of the fire from her, he would have. She had done so much for him and his children in a short time.

"I'm so sorry. I know how hard that must have been for you."

Annie shuddered as though memories inundated her. "I didn't even get to go to my mother's funeral because I was in the burn unit."

It had been important to Ian to go to Zoe's funeral to say goodbye. If he hadn't been able, there was no telling the emotional state he would be in now. "Did your family have a memorial service for her later so you could attend?"

"Yes..." She pulled back, erecting a wall between them. "But I'm not the issue. Jeremy is. I told him because I wanted him to realize I know what he's going through. His life has been changed suddenly, and he has to find ways to deal with it. Until his seizures are under better control, he'll need to be watched more. He's rebelling. I did, too."

Ian clamped his teeth together to keep all his questions about her situation to himself. His inquiries wouldn't be appreciated, and that saddened him. He wanted Annie to share her life with him as he had with her. "So that's the reason he changed his mind about Rex," he finally said.

"I don't know if it was, but when you're hurting like he is, knowing others have survived difficult situations helps. I told him about losing my mother, too. He needs Rex, and I think he'll figure that out once Rex comes to live with him."

Are you all right? The urge to ask her overwhelmed him, but he couldn't. Ian had the feeling Annie didn't share her experience with many, and he tried to respect her privacy.

Her hair, back in its usual place now, effectively covered her visible scars. The doctor in him wanted to examine them and see what he could do. Did she see her scars as a penance because she'd survived the fire and her mother hadn't? Why hadn't she done more to diminish them? There were creams and makeup that could help. Her ear could be replaced with a prosthetic one. Was it money? Or something else? As the thoughts swirled through his mind, Ian realized he needed more information, but he didn't feel he could ask her. Maybe after she'd worked for him longer, he could get her the help she needed.

"At least tomorrow I can reassure him that his mother didn't have epilepsy and didn't die from a seizure. When are you going to tell the others?"

"When the time is right. I don't want them

to think it's a big deal. I've learned to accept my scars."

"There are some procedures that would mask—"

"Don't. They are part of me now."

"But you can get help."

Annie bolted to her feet. "I can't afford the medical procedures. End of conversation."

Ian knew when to back off, but that didn't mean he would forget it. He could help her. He needed to help her. "I shouldn't have overstepped my boundaries. In a short time, you've done so much for my family that..." The anger in her expression stilled the rest of his sentence. "I'd better return to my house."

On the short walk to the back door into the kitchen, Ian couldn't shake the idea there was something he could do for Annie. It was hard for him to turn away from someone in need, especially someone who had been there for him. Someone he cared about. Maybe once they got to know each other better, she would be willing to listen to what he could arrange for her.

"That went well with Rex today." Ian pulled away from Caring Canines the next day, still not sure how to approach his son about his mother.

At a four-way stop sign on the highway into Cimarron City, Ian glanced toward Jeremy. His son had been active in the training with Rex rather than a bystander. That might not have happened without Annie sharing her ordeal. When they'd talked in her apartment last night, Ian had gotten a glimpse of what had made her who she was today. She'd acted as though she'd accepted what happened. Ian wasn't so sure she really had, and if not, she could never live her life fully.

He pulled out into the intersection. "I had a talk with Annie yesterday. She told me about when you saw your mother have a seizure right before she died. Jeremy, I want you to know that a seizure didn't cause her death. Not at all. She died from a second stroke." His voice quavered with the memory.

"I miss her."

"So do I, but I know that your mom would want you to move on. She would want the best for you." *And for me.* Ian needed to listen to his own words. Zoe wouldn't want him mourning her for the rest of his life. "Son, you can talk to me any time you want about anything. In fact, at our next family meeting, we should talk about your mother. I don't want you to think you can't."

"Did...Annie...tell you anything else?"

"Yes. She told me about her scars."

Jeremy blew a long breath out. "Good. I didn't know how long I could keep that a secret. Why does she hide them?"

"Probably for the same reason you don't want anyone to see you having a seizure."

"She's embarrassed? She thinks someone will make fun of her?"

Ian nodded.

"But she's a grown-up."

"Age doesn't have anything to do with it."

Jeremy was silent for a long moment, then asked, "What do you do when someone makes fun of you?"

"Did they?"

"No, not yet."

"If it happens, ignore them." Had someone made fun of Annie? He hated the thought that she might have been ridiculed because of her scars.

"How?"

"Walk away. Once you engage them you feed into what they want. Most people make fun of a person because they are scared what might happen to them or they're trying to get attention."

"There's a guy at school like that."

"Have you ever told your teacher?"

"I'm not a tattletale."

"There are times you need to speak up." Ian pulled into the garage.

"How am I supposed to know when?"

"If it's hurting someone in any way, you should let your teacher know. Has this guy ever bothered you?"

Jeremy shook his head. "But if I have a seizure, he will."

"Let me know if he does."

His son climbed from the Lexus.

"Jeremy, will you?"

He sighed. "Maybe." Then he hurried toward the door to the breezeway.

At a slower pace Ian made his way into the house, not sure how successful he'd been with talking with his son. Only time would tell.

When he came into the kitchen, Annie was drawing a star over April 27. She looked back at him and smiled. "Joshua told me I forgot to mark his birthday."

"He won't let anyone forget." Ian started across the room but stopped when he spied a vase full of red tulips. "Where did these come from?"

"I think I have a secret admirer. They were in my car seat this morning when I drove the kids to school." She finished the yellow star and faced him. "Any idea who?"

"A secret admirer?"

"Perhaps."

Or...something else. "I'll be right back to help with supper."

Ian entered his office and put his briefcase on his desk then went to the window on the left side of the house. His red tulips were gone. Cut. He laughed and decided not to say anything to Annie.

A week later Annie entered the dining room to find Joshua standing at the window looking out front. Daisy sat next to him. "Are you watching for Jeremy and your dad?"

"Yes. So is Daisy."

"She is?" Smiling, Annie crossed to Joshua and sat in a chair near him. "Your sisters are upstairs watching from Jade's room."

"Yup, but I'm gonna get outside faster."

"Not without me."

A few days earlier he'd darted across a parking lot at school without looking. A woman had had to slam on her brakes and barely missed him. His teacher had still been shaken when Annie had picked up Joshua from school.

He hung his head. "I know."

Annie peered out the window and saw Ian's car turn in to the long driveway. "They're here."

Joshua started to run for the front door, but Annie caught up with him and stopped his mad dash. She offered her hand to him as Jade and Jasmine stormed down the stairs.

Ian pulled into the garage but left the door up. By the time Jeremy climbed from the car and Rex followed, they were surrounded by everyone wanting to pet the new dog.

Ian joined Annie. He looked tired. He'd left the house early that morning for surgery. "How did it go?"

"Jeremy was actually excited about getting Rex." Ian leaned close and murmured, "Although he tried to hide it."

His whispered words tickled the side of her face, creating goose bumps on her arms. "I've noticed he's been researching black Labs and service dogs. I'm not sure he'll admit it, but I think he's glad he went ahead with getting Rex."

"Did you get everything set up for Joshua's birthday party Saturday?"

"I've invited his classmates and have the All-Star Combo bounce house being delivered that morning. They'll be able to jump, climb and slide."

"And they'll be exhausted when they leave."

Annie backed away as the children left the garage with both dogs. "I think Daisy and Rex will be the hit of the party."

"I think so, too. Has Jeremy changed his mind about taking Rex to school?"

"No, but give him time," she said, "especially when he sees the younger kids wanting to know all about Rex."

"I'm praying he doesn't have an incident at school before that." Ian strolled with Annie toward the front door.

"Do you see how Daisy follows Rex? Emma told me they were buddies at Caring Canines. She's been a good choice for the kids."

Ian held the door open for Annie. "Have you gotten anything else from your secret admirer?" A gleam lit his eyes.

"Yes, how did you know?" It couldn't be Ian. She felt as though one of the kids was behind the gifts she'd been receiving the past week.

He shrugged. *Does he know something?* "A candy bar, my favorite kind. I remember all of us talking at dinner the other night about what we liked, and surprise, I had one on my seat in the Explorer this morning."

"I'm sure this secret admirer will come forward eventually." Ian looked away. "I've got some literature you might be interested in. I meant to give it to you last night, but with the kids going to all their activities and then getting them ready for bed, I forgot."

As the four children ascended the stairs,

Annie tried to decide if she should point-blank ask him who her secret admirer was. "Literature? If it's not a suspense story, I won't be reading it."

"This isn't a book. I'll be right back." Ian headed toward his office on the ground floor.

What was he up to? When she saw him carrying a brochure, Annie's stomach tightened. Something told her she didn't want to see it. She straightened, tensing as though preparing for a hit.

"This is about prosthetic ears." Ian handed it to her.

Annie stared at it but wouldn't take it. "I can't afford it, so there's no reason to read it." Anger welled in her, quickly replaced by hurt. Why couldn't he accept her, flaws and all? "I'm going to check on the kids then start dinner. I don't need help this evening." She started for the stairs.

"Wait, Annie. I didn't mean to make you mad."

She rotated toward him. "I'm not angry. Disappointed."

She hurried up the steps, needing to put space between them. She had set out trying to hide her scars with her long hair covering her ear and turtleneck shirts even in summer, but she didn't like being the center of attention or the idea people thought she needed to be fixed.

After checking on the children and dogs, Annie prepared a Mexican chicken casserole that would be easy to serve without her here. Then she called her sister and told her she was coming over. By her own choice she had very few days or nights off, but this evening when the family sat down for dinner, she was leaving to see Amanda.

Annie paced the back porch at Amanda's. "Nothing is wrong with me. Why does he want to fix me?"

"I'm getting whiplash with your pacing. Sit so we can have a conversation. People have said things to you before. You don't usually get this worked up, so why are you getting upset now?"

Annie stopped in front of her twin. "Ian was supposed to be different."

"He was? Did you let him know that?"

"I told him I couldn't afford it. That should have been the end. It wasn't. He gave me a brochure about a prosthetic ear. Why?"

"Did you ask him?"

"Well, no, not exactly. I told him again I didn't have the money then handed the brochure back." Annie sat across from her sister.

"He's a plastic surgeon. That's the kind of

thing he does for a living. I once dated a dentist who kept staring at my teeth. He told me that's the first thing he checks out on a person."

"So since I told him last week, he's been trying to figure out a way to make me better." Annie heard the sarcasm pour from her voice, mingling with hurt.

"I know we've talked about this before, but you usually shut it down. Annie, why won't you look into treatment for your scars? You were burned almost fourteen years ago. There have been so many advances in medicine. I don't see why you don't at least investigate your options and how much each one costs. You know we'd help you as much as possible."

Annie rose and began pacing again, her hands fisted at her sides. "That isn't the kind of support I came here for. You of all people should understand."

Amanda planted herself in Annie's path. "Understand what?"

Didn't anyone understand what she'd gone through? "It's my reparation for Mom."

"You still believe that?" Amanda's voice had risen several decibels. "That's the last thing Mom would ever want. If that's what you believe, I know the emotional scars will never totally go away. It was an *accident*, Annie. Accept that and forgive yourself."

Each word her sister said struck her like a slap, stinging and hurting. "It's not that easy. Forgive and forget." Annie snapped her fingers. "Just like that. Tell myself and it's done."

"I didn't say it was easy. If God can forgive you, why can't you forgive yourself? I think that's why you won't do anything about your scars."

Annie charged to the sliding glass doors and headed toward the front exit. "I needed sympathy, not accusations. Good night."

She sat in her car, clutching the steering wheel until her hands ached. Annie thought the one person who would understand was her twin. A van passed her, its headlights illuminating the interior of her vehicle. She caught a glimpse of herself in the rearview mirror, the edges of her scars peeking out from behind her hair. The sight taunted her.

Annie looked down and tried to compose herself before returning to the McGregors' house. She released her hold on the steering wheel and flexed her hands. A tiny voice inside her kept insisting she leave Ian before she began to care about him. Who was she kidding? She cared about him now. Hadn't she learned her lesson with David?

For a brief time Annie had thought a man could overlook her scars, but David's disgust had destroyed that dream. She'd finally started dating and begun to let down her guard with David. When she'd showed him the scars, he hadn't been able to get away from her fast enough.

But Annie had promised the children she'd be there for them. They'd lost so many caretakers in two years. She couldn't leave now, especially with Jeremy fighting to accept himself. He was fragile, warming to her and yet still holding himself back. Jasmine, too.

Annie finally started the car and drove back to her apartment. She'd get a good night's sleep and be all right tomorrow. The next few days wouldn't be as hectic as the weekend with the birthday party.

She parked in the three-car garage and rounded the corner to climb the stairs to her apartment. For a few seconds her heartbeat galloped at the sight of a man sitting on the bottom step. She gasped.

"Sorry, I should have said something."

"Where's your truck?"

Her youngest brother pushed to a standing position. "Being towed to the dealer. I had Ken drop me off here so I could borrow your car for the next couple of days."

Annie jammed both fists onto her waist.

"Have you ever heard of calling before assuming you could take my car?"

"I texted you. I thought maybe you were putting the kids down, so I told your boss that I'd wait for you on the stairs."

Annie dug into her purse and found her dead cell phone. "I forgot to charge it last night." She assessed her brother for a long moment. "I guess you can use my car."

"Where have you been? Ian didn't know where you were."

"Out. None of your business or his. And if you persist with the questions, I won't loan you my Honda." She placed the keys into his hand and punched the garage door opener. "Did you have a wreck?" she finally asked.

"No, the brakes failed, and I went over a curb. I finally stopped inches from hitting a big tree trunk."

Ian suddenly came into the garage from the breezeway but hung back. Annie didn't have to look to know he was staring at her. A flutter zipped through her at the brief sight of him.

She peered at Charlie, trying to ignore Ian's presence but failing miserably. "Let me know when you can return it."

"Will do."

After her brother backed her car out of the garage, she hit the button on the door opener to close it. Maybe Ian, still in the garage, would get the point she wasn't ready to talk to him.

But what if something had happened to one of the children? Annie started to punch the button again to open it, but Ian beat her to it.

He strode toward her. Worry lines etched his forehead.

"Ian, is something wrong with Jeremy?"

"No. The kids are fine and asleep and so are the dogs—Rex with Jeremy and Daisy with Joshua."

"So he finally persuaded Daisy to sleep with him."

"I think the girls came to an agreement with their little brother. Daisy is going to rotate where she sleeps."

"That seems reasonable."

"But not what I did earlier. I assumed you'd want to look at that information, never thinking of the cost. I'm sorry."

What tension was left in her body melted away. It was hard to stay mad at Ian because he did have good intentions, and when he looked at her scars, it hadn't been with revulsion but like a doctor examining an injury. But still.

"Ian, I am who I am. It's totally my decision what I do."

But Ian hadn't said anything her family hadn't...Annie had her life mapped out just fine, and she helped people. That was her purpose, not to be a wife and mother.

"I didn't want to go to bed without making amends. You're important to this family."

"I'm glad, Ian." *I want to be needed.*

"Good night," Ian said and walked to the door to the breezeway.

Annie made her way toward the staircase on the side of the garage, trying to focus on all the things she needed to get done before fifteen children descended on the house on Saturday. She didn't get far because her thoughts always returned to Ian. If he ever decided to remarry, he'd make some woman a good husband. That realization didn't sit well with her as she mounted the steps.

Chapter Nine

On Friday Annie picked up the phone. “The McGregors’ residence.”

“This is Mrs. Haskell, Jeremy’s teacher. May I speak with Annie Knight?”

“This is she.” Her heart began beating double-time. Something was wrong.

“I tried Dr. McGregor’s office, and they said he was in surgery. Your name is the other one on the contact sheet.”

“Is Jeremy okay?”

“He’s with the nurse. He had a seizure on the playground after lunch. Physically he’s fine, but he was upset when he saw the other kids around him. He refused to come back to class, and the nurse told me he fell asleep on their cot.”

“I’ll come pick him up.”

“Under these circumstances, I think that would be best.”

After Annie retrieved Rex from the backyard, she drove toward Will Rogers Elementary. Her cell phone rang, and she saw it was Ian. "I'm almost at Jeremy's school," he said. "He had a seizure. The teacher called and left a message for me. When I got out of surgery, an aide told me."

"He's at the nurse's office."

"Meet you there."

Annie pulled into the parking lot, took Rex out of the backseat and hooked up his leash. Not half a minute later, Ian pulled in next to her. She waited for him, then they walked to the entrance together.

"Good idea about Rex," Ian said. "I didn't insist on Jeremy's taking Rex to school, but I will now." He opened the door.

While Annie and Ian signed in at the office, she said, "We have the weekend to see if he'll come to the conclusion on his own. I brought Rex to remind Jeremy what the dog can do for him. And I have a feeling Jeremy could use Rex for comfort, although I doubt he'll admit it. It upset him that the kids on the playground saw him. His teacher said he freaked out."

"It's time we encourage him to talk about his epilepsy with the other children. Rex could help with that."

At the nurse's office, Ian asked what happened and how long the seizure had lasted while Annie took Rex to the room where the cots were. When they entered, Jeremy was curled on his side, his eyes closed. Annie sat in the chair between the beds with Rex between her and Jeremy's cot.

Ian went in and sat on the other bed, whispering, "The nurse said he went to sleep right away. He's been here about forty minutes. His seizure lasted around three minutes. That was an estimate from the teacher's assistant on the playground. Jeremy fell down on a soft patch of grass, and she couldn't feel any bumps or see any cuts."

"What do you want to do?"

"Take him home. He'll be wiped. That's the longest seizure he's had that I know of." Ian stood and stooped next to his son. "Jeremy." He gently shook the child's shoulder.

Jeremy's eyes blinked open and he looked right at his dad then closed them.

"Son, I'm taking you home. Can you walk?"

No response.

"Then, I'll carry you." Ian slipped his arms under his child's body and hefted him up against his chest.

"I'll get the doors." Annie scurried around Ian, holding Rex's leash, and walked ahead of them out to the Lexus. "Are you going back to work?"

"No. My surgeries went faster than I thought they would."

"I'm going to run one errand, then it will be time for me to pick up the other children."

"I'll see you back at the house in a while."

Annie opened her driver's door while Ian placed Jeremy in the backseat of his Lexus, and Rex climbed in with his son.

Ian straightened. His gaze held her like an embrace. "Thanks for coming, Annie. It's good to know I have someone to rely on." His voice thickened, and he swallowed hard.

"I'm doing what is needed," Annie murmured, wanting to look away, but the sheen in his eyes riveted her.

Ian loved his children, and to see them hurt and vulnerable had to be hard for him. Annie wasn't their parent, but she struggled with her emotions more than when she worked for the others. She couldn't compartmentalize her feelings as she had before. It would be difficult to leave the children—Ian.

Not a word was spoken for half a minute. Annie couldn't have moved if she'd wanted to.

Then Ian's cell phone rang, breaking the connection. Annie hurried and slid into the Ford Explorer. She still had an errand to run, but the whole way to the store, she couldn't shake the idea that something had happened back there. Something had changed between them.

"I can't believe my youngest is five. It goes by fast, especially when you're running to keep up with him." Ian stood next to Annie on the sidewalk, watching ten four-and five-year-olds jumping, sliding and climbing all over the bounce house that took up a good part of his front yard. "I warned the neighbors it might be a tad noisy today."

"You think? I should have given earplugs to Amanda." Annie laughed and raised her voice over the shouting, with Joshua's ten friends and the twins each having one, as well.

"And us. Did you see Jade and Jasmine looking between you and your twin earlier?"

"We dressed exactly alike on purpose. I thought it would be fun to try to fool your daughters."

Ian turned toward the woman beside him and studied her. "Are you Amanda?"

"What do you think?" A twinkle danced in her eyes.

Ian glanced toward her sister by the door to the bounce house. Joshua ran up to her, grinning from ear to ear, and threw his arms around her. Ian returned his attention to the woman standing with him, catching her running her finger under the collar of her turtleneck shirt. "You are definitely Amanda."

"What gave it away? Annie and I are pretty good at changing places."

"You aren't used to wearing a turtleneck."

"True. We fooled your daughters, though. Annie is going to save telling them until later."

"But not Joshua. That hug was for Annie. She made today special for him." Lately there had been a lot of special moments for Ian's family because of Annie.

Amanda tilted her head and scrutinized him. "You like her. I'm glad because I think she's terrific, too. She has a gift with children, and they gravitate to her. I thought Annie would be a teacher. But she wanted to do something more one-on-one."

"I'm glad she decided that. For the past two weeks, my family has finally started settling into a routine. Before Annie, no matter what I did, I couldn't seem to get it together."

"Four children take a lot of coordinating. Annie had the best example. Our mom was always there for us. We knew what she expected, and we knew our boundaries."

Ian smiled. "Zoe and then Aunt Louise always held the fort. When they passed away, I was left unprepared."

"Sounds as though Annie came in the nick of time."

Ian watched Annie among the children in the bounce house, laughing as loud as they were. She gave him hope again. When he'd opened the door to her that first day, he had been desperate. Ian didn't like chaos any more than his kids did. He wanted to help her, too. "Amanda, why won't Annie do anything about her scars?"

"She's become good at hiding them."

"But I think something could be done to diminish them. At least on her face. And certainly her ear could either be reconstructed, or she could have a prosthetic one."

"The ones on her neck and ear aren't nearly as bad as the one across her chest. But in answer to your question, I can't say. If Annie wants you to know, she'll tell you."

Ian faced Amanda, not surprised by her answer. "I understand. You two are very close, like Jade and Jasmine."

"Annie doesn't trust easily. After the accident she discovered who her real friends were. It's sad how some people view beauty only outwardly. But then you should know that—your business revolves around appearance."

"There's more to being a plastic surgeon than cosmetic procedures," Ian said. "The part I love best is the reconstructive surgery. My little brother had a cleft lip, and he got teased to the point he didn't want to go to school. Surgery changed his life."

"Wouldn't it be nice if people would just accept us for what we are? God does." Amanda checked her watch. "I'm going to relieve Annie. I need to work off that piece of cake."

Ian scanned the children. Jeremy had never come outside after Joshua opened his presents, and everyone had cake and ice cream. He'd said he would. After making sure everything was running smoothly, Ian went inside and found his eldest son sitting on the staircase with Rex next to him.

"I thought you were coming outside. Joshua will wonder where you are."

"What if I have a seizure like yesterday?"

"We're here to help you. You'll be okay. You can't hide in the house forever."

His service dog moved closer and laid his head in Jeremy's lap.

"You've got Rex. He's there to help. Remember what he did that evening at Caring Canines?"

"But on the playground everyone was staring at me." Jeremy chewed on his lower lip.

Ian sat next to his son. Had Annie gone through this after her accident? "Because they didn't know about your seizures. Maybe you need to share it with them. Rex can help you."

"What if someone laughs at me?"

"Then, he isn't a friend. You need to ignore him. I hope you'll take Rex to school on Monday."

Jeremy stroked his dog's head. "I don't know."

"I know Joshua's friends would love to get to know Rex better. Come on. I'll show you." Ian stood and waited.

When his son rose, Ian filled his lungs with a deep breath. Outside, when Jeremy strolled toward the bounce house, several kids came up to him. Before long three more joined them. Jeremy began demonstrating some of the tricks Rex could do. Relief flowed through Ian.

"I'm glad you could talk him into getting out of the house," Annie said from behind. "I tried earlier, but he didn't know if he should."

Ian rotated toward Annie. "This is a good place for him to practice sharing his service dog with others. The more comfortable he is, the more likely he will take Rex to school willingly."

"Joshua asked me this morning after breakfast if he could take Daisy."

"He said something to me, too, right before the party. Obviously you didn't give him the right answer."

Annie chuckled. “Kids don’t think adults compare notes. Amanda and I used to do that all the time with our parents.” She looked around. “Where are Jade and Jasmine?”

“I don’t know. Their two friends are still here, so they can’t be too far away. At least I don’t have to worry about them—unlike Joshua when he disappears for any length of time.”

“I think those older girls are flirting with Jeremy,” Annie observed. “The other kids are going back to play in the bounce house, but the twins’ friends are hanging on to every word Jeremy is saying.”

“He’s blushing. I didn’t know Jeremy could do that. Want to walk around and look for the twins?”

“Let’s check behind the bounce house.”

“Over by Jeremy? Maybe we can eavesdrop.” Annie tried, but she couldn’t contain her grin.

“I think that’s a good suggestion. Jade and Jasmine could be on the other side of that monstrosity in my yard.”

Annie started forward. “I told you it would be big. Quit complaining so we can hear what the girls and Jeremy are saying as we walk by.”

“Why, Annie Knight, I never thought you were capable of such underhanded behavior.” Lately he’d noticed he’d smiled and laughed more than anytime the past year. And he was sure it was because of Annie. She was having an effect on the children—but also on him.

"When it comes to protecting children, you do what you have to," Annie replied.

Ian's laughter caused his son and the two girls to glance their way.

Annie jabbed Ian playfully in the side and whispered, "So much for being subtle." They kept walking.

"Did you hear he was explaining what his service dog does?" Ian asked as they circled the bounce house.

"Dad, Annie, look at me." Joshua went down the slide headfirst.

"Joshua, I'm glad that landing is cushioned. And yes, I heard," she told Ian. Annie came to a halt, staring at the front porch, then she burst out laughing.

Ian swung his attention to what she was looking at. His two daughters were coming toward them, dressed exactly alike and wearing the same hairstyle. "It's rare to see Jade wearing a dress. I'm surprised Jasmine talked her into it."

"When it comes to clothes, Jasmine is adamant about what she puts on. Jade couldn't care less." Annie waved at the two girls. "They won't fool me. The minute they start talking they'll give themselves away. They haven't mastered the art of switching places the way Amanda and I have." Annie nodded toward them. "For instance, they walk differently."

"I never thought about that, but it's true."

As Annie greeted the twins by name, the flush to their cheeks revealed she was right. In a short time, Annie had come to know his family well, Ian reflected. In some ways she knew them better than he did, which was disconcerting. He'd been lost in grief the past two years and had distanced himself from his children. That would change today.

Sunday evening, after they'd held the family meeting and the children had gone to bed, Annie left for the night. But instead of going to her apartment, she sat on a lounge chair on the patio to enjoy the crisp, cool spring air with a sky lit with thousands of stars. This had been a weekend full of surprises. First, Annie had thought for sure she could fool Ian when Amanda and she switched roles, but she hadn't for long. That stunned her. Did Ian know her that well? The thought that he did excited and scared her at the same time.

Annie pushed away thoughts of men and focused on another surprise. Jeremy not only brought Rex outside at the birthday party, but he'd taken him to church, too. Both were good dry runs for tomorrow. Tonight at supper, he'd announced Rex was going to school with him.

But the biggest revelation was today when Annie had spent most of the day with her family and all she could think about was Ian and his children. She'd wanted them there, too. Her dad encouraged her to ask them to come for Memorial Day at the lake, and she was definitely considering it.

The sound of the sliding glass doors opening startled her. Annie twisted around to find Ian coming out of the house toward her. Although she'd relished the quiet, his presence sent a thrill through her. She needed to put a stop to that—but at the moment she didn't know how.

"I was checking that the doors were locked and caught sight of you out here. Mind if I join you?"

"This is your house."

"But this is your downtime."

"Haven't you figured out by now that except for church and family, I have no life beyond my job?" Annie smiled. Until she'd come to Ian's house, that had been true. But when she was with Ian and his family, she didn't think of herself as an employee. Annie slid her eyes closed for a few seconds and tried to change the direction of her thoughts.

"So that's why you come back early on Sunday and join us for dinner."

"Well, that and I don't have to cook the meal." And Annie enjoyed the family meetings—each one showed progress toward a good working model.

"I thought you liked to cook."

"I do, but it's nice to be pampered every once in a while."

"I'll have to remember that." Ian took the lounge next to her.

Only inches apart. His proximity revved her heartbeat, and she shivered.

"Cold?"

"No, I'm fine." *As soon as I quit reacting to you being this close to me.* "Tonight is so lovely I decided to spend some time out here."

"I have a feeling the quiet is what lured you."

"You're probably right, after spending today with my large family. I think every niece and nephew was there today. Usually a couple are missing."

"What are their ages?"

"When everyone is present, their ages are two to fifteen, but in seven months there will be a baby. Amanda told me she's eight weeks pregnant. Her first, and I'm excited! I've had plenty of practice with all the stages children go through, but the baby stage is my favorite."

"What about having your own? You would be such a good mother."

Annie tensed, relieved that in the dark Ian couldn't read her expression. The subject always brought a momentary pang of regret and pain. Because of her forgetfulness that night at the cabin, she'd been denied the one thing she'd always wanted: to be a mother. If she could relive that moment she lit the candle, her life would be totally different today.

"Annie?" Ian clasped her hand.

"I can't have children. When the beam fell across my midsection, it caused some internal injuries." The words slipped out before Annie could take them back. Only her family and her doctor knew that information. Why was she telling Ian? It wasn't his concern, but she found herself sharing more with him than any other outsider.

"I'm sorry. I shouldn't…" For a long moment Ian didn't say anything.

Annie swung her legs over the side of the chaise longue and sat up. "You were making an observation, and I appreciate your thinking I would be a good mother. I accepted the fact I wouldn't be able to years ago." But she could still remember that day when the doctor had told her. Something had died inside her then. God had other plans for her life.

Ian leaned forward. "I shouldn't have asked. It's none of my business, but I don't think of us as employer and employee. I've enjoyed getting to know you. I consider you a friend. You're easy to talk to. And I don't know what I would have done about Jeremy without you. For six months I've felt overwhelmed. I don't now."

Annie knew her other employers had appreciated her services, but their words had never affected her the way Ian's did. A glow from deep within spread to encompass her whole body. "I'm glad I could help" was all she could think to say.

"It was a great day when you came to interview for the job."

Annie rose. "It's time to call it a night."

When Ian stood so close she could smell his scent of lime aftershave, her breathing quickened. She wanted to forget her past and focus only on this man, this moment alone with him.

"I'm taking the kids and Rex to school tomorrow morning," he told her. "I want you to sleep in and enjoy the time off. You deserve it."

"But I don't—"

"You've hardly taken any time off, so no argument."

His nearness made her heartbeat accelerate. "But what about breakfast?" The question came out in a breathless rush.

"A bowl of cereal will be fine. Okay?"

Annie nodded, transfixed by his heart-pounding look.

Ian bent his head toward hers, his hands grasping her upper arms. When his lips hovered over hers, she wanted to melt against him.

Chapter Ten

Ian knew he shouldn't kiss her, but he couldn't resist. His lips whispered across hers, giving her time to pull away if she wanted. When she didn't, he slanted his mouth over hers and deepened their connection. When he pulled back slightly and looked at her, he saw a woman who had become so important to him in such a short time. He wanted more. Ian kissed her forehead, eyes, the tip of her nose and then her mouth again. When his hands delved into her thick hair, his fingers touched her scars. He didn't care about them.

Suddenly she tore from his embrace, backing away. As she encountered the lounge chair, the sound of it scooting across the patio filled the air. In the shadows created by the light from the den, panic lined her face. She frantically combed her hair over her scars.

Annie glanced down at the askew chaise longue for a few seconds before her wide-eyed gaze reconnected with his. "It's been a long week. Thanks for the morning off. Good night."

"Annie, I didn't mean—"

"I know you didn't mean to kiss me. Why would you?"

As she started to leave, Ian caught her hand. "First, I wanted to kiss you, but I didn't mean to scare you or make you mad. I'm sorry."

Annie tugged her hand free then hurried toward the side of the garage. Ian watched her escape. She didn't realize how beautiful she was. She was using her scars as a barrier between herself and others. He wanted to change that.

Lord, how do I get her to see her beauty?

Annie didn't stop running until she was inside her apartment—then she collapsed back against the door. She should never have responded to Ian's kiss. But when his lips touched hers, that was all she could think about.

He wanted to kiss me.

Why?

Gratitude. That's all it could be. If Ian could see my scarred body, he would run the other way. That's why I keep my distance from men.

Annie could leave, find another job, but she wouldn't do that to the children. She just needed to toughen her resolve to keep her relationship with Ian as employer/employee. No more.

But the lingering feel of his lips against hers mocked that decision. Annie wanted Ian to kiss her again.

The next morning a bang against her door drew Annie out of her bedroom. "Just a minute." She tied the sash to her robe as she padded across her apartment to see who had disturbed her morning to sleep in.

She peered out the peephole, but no one was on the landing. Then another bang sounded as though someone was kicking against the wood. She eased the door open to find Joshua, still wearing his pajamas, his forehead furrowed.

"What's wrong?"

"Daddy is sick."

"Did he tell you to come get me?"

"No, but I heard him coughing and coughing and coughing. He needs you."

A vivid memory of the kiss they'd shared the night before flashed into her mind. Annie quickly dismissed that thought and said, "Come in, Joshua. Let me get dressed."

Joshua shifted from one foot to the other, his gaze zooming in on her neck. "Didja hurt yourself?"

Annie brushed her hair forward as much as

possible and threw up the collar on her robe. "Not lately. Be right back."

Annie hurried away from Joshua before he started asking more questions. She still hadn't told him or the girls. The time hadn't been right yet. After throwing on a pair of jeans and a red turtleneck, Annie returned to the living room.

Joshua was gone.

She hastened outside, remembering that time he'd tried to fly off the railing. But the landing was empty. She rushed down the stairs and rounded the corner to find Joshua picking—or rather uprooting—some lilies.

"Joshua, you were supposed to wait for me."

"You didn't tell me to." He grinned and handed her the flowers, roots and all.

Annie thought back to what she'd said and he was right—technically. She knew better than not to spell out what she expected. "Thanks for the flowers, but you should leave them in the ground next time."

"They're pretty like you." He wiped his dirty hands on his pajamas.

Annie was at a loss for words. Was Joshua behind the red tulips, the candy bar and the other little gifts? No, he couldn't be. Later she would replant them and hope the lilies survived, but for now she needed to see about Ian. "Let's go."

When she and the five-year-old entered the kitchen, Ian was pouring a cup of coffee, his face white and haggard-looking. Suddenly he sneezed then starting coughing.

When he turned his red eyes on her, he said, "Annie, you aren't supposed to be here."

"And you shouldn't be out of bed. Joshua told me you were sick, and he's right."

"No, he isn't. This is just allergies. Spring is the worst time for me. That's what I get for spending time outside at night." He quirked a half grin. "But I'm glad I did. It was worth it."

Annie stamped down the rising warmth in her face and concentrated on the situation at hand. "Are you sure that's all it is—allergies?" She put the lilies next to the sink.

"Positive. I'm a doctor. I should know."

Turning away, Annie rolled her eyes. "Since I'm here, I'll at least fix breakfast and help get the children ready for school."

"Sure. I need to make sure the others are up." Ian shuffled toward the doorway, leaving his full cup of coffee on the counter.

Annie started to say something but decided not to. Coffee wasn't the best thing to drink when a person was coming down with something. She wasn't so sure it was just his allergies. Water was much better.

"Joshua, you should go get dressed. I'll have breakfast ready in fifteen minutes."

Ian paused in the doorway as if he'd finally noticed the lilies on the counter. He gestured toward the flowers. "What happened to them?"

"I gave them to Annie." Joshua zipped past his dad into the hallway.

"Oh." Ian continued out of the kitchen.

Annie quickly prepared French toast and set the table. When she set the pitcher of orange juice on the table, she stepped back, satisfied with what she'd done in a short time. She punched the intercom to announce breakfast, but a movement in the doorway caught her attention.

Jasmine, with a huge pout on her face, stood barefoot, her blouse ripped, her hair a wild mess.

"What happened?"

"I can't go to school today. I have nothing to wear, and my hair is awful."

"I'm sure we can find something for you to wear to school." Annie started for the hallway.

Jasmine blocked the door. "No, I don't want to go to school. I haven't missed much school this year. I don't need to go today."

"Are you sick?"

"I have a headache." Jasmine thought for a

few seconds and added, "And a stomachache. I might throw up any second."

Jade came up behind her sister. "She isn't sick. One of the popular girls said she was too fat on Friday."

Jasmine punched her in the arm as Jade passed her. She faked a cough. "I got it from Dad."

As Joshua entered the kitchen wearing the clothes he'd laid out the night before, Annie spied Jeremy and Rex coming down the hall. "Jeremy, please make sure your younger brother and sister eat, then brush their teeth and get ready to leave."

Jeremy looked at her for a moment then grinned. "Sure. You two heard Annie. I'm the boss."

Annie took Jasmine's hand and led her toward the staircase. "If you have a fever, you can stay home. Otherwise you're going."

Jasmine stopped dead in her tracks. "I can't go. You don't know what it's like to have someone say something about how you look to everyone."

The words hit Annie with a truth she'd been avoiding. She paused on the step and knew this was the time. She sat and patted the place next to her. "Jasmine, I could tell you that what someone says about you only hurts you if you let it. When I was young I did that. I let others control my actions. I still do." More than she realized.

"But I'm not fat, am I?"

Annie shook her head and shifted to face the young girl. "Absolutely not."

"I don't know why she said that. I thought we were friends."

"I don't know why, either. Maybe she's hurting inside, and she thinks by saying something hurtful to someone else it will make her feel better. It won't in the long run."

Suddenly Annie felt fifteen again—the day she returned to school after the fire. Nothing had prepared her for that—feeling damaged, freakish. Annie had seen it in some people's eyes, and it had cut through her.

"Are you okay?"

Annie dragged herself away from the past and focused on the child who needed her help. "When I was in high school, I was in a fire and was burned. Most of the scars I can hide under my clothes—" she lifted her hair on the right side to reveal her partial ear and disfigurement "—but not this. My hair was short then because of the fire, but as soon as I could I began using it to hide the scars. I didn't want kids to talk about how ugly I was. I let them control my life and what I did."

Tears swam in Jasmine's eyes. "You aren't ugly. You are…you." She hugged Annie. "You care about us."

Annie put her arms around the child, savoring the moment. "And that's how I feel about you. You aren't fat. And even if you were, you are you. Who am I to judge you? Friends won't. They care about us, flaws and all."

As she said those words to Jasmine, their meaning began to sink in. Yes, Annie had scars, but that wasn't who she was inside. If others couldn't accept them, that was their problem, not hers.

"What am I supposed to do about Kayla?"

"Nothing. Go to school and act as though what she said didn't bother you. Words can hurt but only when we give them power to." Annie cupped the girl's face. "Then after school, we'll all go get an ice cream cone. I know how much you love it. So do I. Now, Jasmine, do I still need to take your temperature?"

Jasmine shook her head, swiped her tears away and hopped up. "I'll get ready."

"Good. I'll fix you something to eat on the go." The sound of coughing drifted to Annie. "I have a feeling I'll be taking you this morning."

She walked with Jasmine to the second floor but headed for Ian's room. She knocked and waited. When he opened the door, he used it for support. He was dressed, but his shirttail hung out of his pants and he was barefoot. Without a word, Annie laid her palm against his forehead and felt heat beneath her fingers.

"You can't go to work. You've got a fever. I don't think your patients would appreciate you like this."

"I came to that realization, but I was trying at least to take the kids to school. Then I can come back home and collapse on the bed."

"I'm taking the children, and you're getting back in bed. When I return, I'll check to see if you need anything."

"But you were supposed to have the morning off."

"Not today. Maybe some other time after you're well." Annie gently nudged Ian back toward his bed. "I've got everything under control. Make sure you drink plenty of fluids."

"I'm a doctor, and I know what to do."

"This from a man who should have never gotten out of bed in the first place." Annie left his room, glancing back to make sure he was following her directions. He was, his eyes drifting closed.

Ian's head alternated between pounding and pulsating. Even moving it too fast caused the room to spin. And yet here he sat in his SUV waiting for the prescription his family doctor had written for him when all he wanted to do was lie down in a dark room and sleep. At least he wasn't driving.

Annie took the sack of medication from the cashier then pulled away from the drive-through window. "I have enough time to drop you off then go pick up the children." She glanced toward him. "Now, aren't you glad you went with me to see your friend? The antibiotic will take care of your sinus infection."

Ian removed the medicine bottle from the bag, took out one pill then washed it down with water. "I can't afford to be sick. I have patients to see."

"Your office will reschedule the ones today and tomorrow."

"You're indispensable." Annie wasn't here just for the children but for him, too.

"You would have done what you needed, but it does help to have a backup."

"Especially since I don't have any family nearby to depend on."

"That, I have plenty of."

"I'm jealous," Ian grumbled and laid his head back on the cushion. He looked forward to the moment he could retreat to his room, a luxury he hadn't had in a long time.

"Which brings up Memorial Day. Would you

and your family like to attend our big get-together at the lake? I'd love for you all to meet my extended family. There will be plenty of kids for yours to play with."

"I'd say it sounds great, but right now nothing does. But yes, I think that would be good for the children." *And me.*

Ian had realized since Zoe died he'd isolated himself from friends and even family who lived in South Carolina. Until Annie, he hadn't thought he'd retreated from life, but he had. He'd focused on getting through one day at a time and his work. With Aunt Louise taking care of his children, he hadn't even been that involved with relatives right after his wife died. Ian had been feeling sorry for himself. Zoe had been his college sweetheart, the only girl he had seriously dated. He'd thought he was set for life. Then Zoe had had a stroke followed by another one, and everything had changed.

Then along had come Annie, and life was changing again from the rut his life had become. Ian wanted to find a way to show her his appreciation for going above and beyond in her job, and he'd come up with a way, if he could work out all the details.

He'd had some setbacks, but so had Annie. He wanted her to put her past behind her—

as he was trying to do. Both of them had become too focused on what had been, not on what could be.

Three weeks later, Annie drove to Will Rogers Elementary the last Tuesday before school was out for Super Sports Day. Every class was having a picnic on the playground, then the students would participate in competitions. Jeremy and Ian were going to do a three-legged race while Jade would be putting a potato between her knees and trying to walk from one end of the basketball court to the other. Jasmine and Kayla, paired by their teacher, were going to hold a balloon between their hips and try to make it to the finish line first, while Joshua and Annie would be dancing, then freezing when the music stopped.

Dressed in a blue T-shirt celebrating Super Sports Day, Annie scanned the sea of blue T-shirts before her. She couldn't come without one because according to the kids, everyone would be wearing them. And they were. Even after talking with Jasmine about appearances a few weeks ago, Annie had been hesitant to go without her usual turtleneck at least under her T-shirt. But in the end, she'd realized children learned by example more than words. Annie needed to show Jasmine that what other people said shouldn't control what she felt about herself or how she acted.

Annie, carrying everyone's sack lunches, stopped at the edge of the playground, where she met Ian.

"The trick is to cover all the children today. I'll start with Joshua's class at this end." She pointed to Jade in the third-grade area. "I'll go there next, then to Jasmine and finish with Jeremy with the fourth graders. You do the opposite, and we should meet between Jade and Jasmine's classes."

"Last year they had different grades compete on different days. Whatever possessed them to do it all in one afternoon?"

"Beats me. We'll get a workout for sure. Whether the kids do is still up in the air." Annie glanced from one end of the playground to the other—at least two football fields long.

"I'll take Jeremy and the twins their lunches. See you in a while." Ian strolled toward the area for the third graders.

Since the time Ian had been sick a few weeks ago, Annie had tried to keep a distance between them, but it had been difficult—and she suspected the twins of plotting to get Ian and her alone together. She was sure they were responsible for all those secret admirer gifts. So far she'd managed to foil their plans, but they hadn't let up.

Maybe she needed to talk with them about the impossibility of their dad and her getting together. There would come a time when Ian would be ready to date and possibly marry again. By that time Annie would move on to other children who needed her help. Annie knew she couldn't stay when Ian became serious about a woman. She cared too much to hang around. His kiss had shown that. She still dreamed about it.

Joshua ran to her, throwing his arms around her. "You came!"

Annie tousled his curly blond hair. "Of course. How could I miss dancing with you?"

"Yeah, but when the music stops, we have to stand *real* still. I want to win. If you move we'll hafta sit down."

"I'll try to stay still." She tried to keep a straight face. Joshua was the one always on the move.

When the dance competition was announced, Joshua put on a serious expression, paying attention to everything his teacher said. Then the music started. Holding Annie's hand—they had to remain connected the whole time—he wiggled and twisted, nearly wrenching her arm out of the socket. When the song stopped, Joshua froze, his gaze fixed on her. By the third stop, his body was contorted into a weird position, and he couldn't keep still longer than a second. The teacher pointed to them to sit down.

Joshua walked off with Annie, his shoulders slumped and his head down, while Annie rotated her shoulder. He plopped down on one of the blankets his class had laid out.

"Joshua, you might not have been the last person left standing, but you got some good exercise." Which was the point of Super Sports Day.

Another boy sat near Joshua and stared at Annie. "What's wrong with your neck?" The child pointed at her scars.

Annie had prepared herself for questions from curious children. "I was in a fire."

His eyes got big. "You were? Did a fireman save you?"

"My dad did." A knot swelled into her throat, and Annie swallowed several times, not wanting to think about that day.

"Do they still hurt?"

She shook her head.

By the time she left Joshua, several other children had said something to her about her scars, more curious than anything. When she arrived at Jade's class, Annie felt hopeful about her decision. It took her telling Jasmine to see that she'd been letting a few callous people change how she felt and acted.

Jade's friends were fun and pumped about Super Sports Day. Not one of them asked about her scars, although they had seen them. Annie knew she'd made a good decision to let them show. For fourteen years her life had revolved around what had happened at the fire. Not anymore.

As Annie walked toward Jasmine, she waved to Ian, who made a detour to talk to her, greeting her with a smile. "You look as if you've been enjoying yourself."

"I have. How did you do in the three-legged race?" she asked, trying to ignore how he made her feel when he looked at her as though she was the only person around.

"I think Rex and Jeremy would have done better." His eyes sparkled with merriment.

"That bad?"

"We came in dead last because I kept tripping. Jeremy was a sport about it, although I'm not sure he's stopped laughing yet."

Annie chuckled at the picture that formed in her mind of the race.

"You're laughing, too! I thought you at least would give me sympathy."

"Sorry." Annie struggled to suppress her smile. "How's Rex handling the crowd?"

"He's loving it. While I was there, Jeremy showed him off to tons of people, telling them all about what his dog can do."

Annie glanced in the direction of Jeremy's class and glimpsed the boy and Rex with other children surrounding them. "Rex has been great for him. I heard Jeremy last night before bedtime, telling him his problems."

"What kind of problems?"

"He didn't do well on his math test, and there's a girl bothering him, pestering him about Rex all the time."

Ian sighed. "Those kinds of problems I can handle, whereas Jasmine is still having trouble with Kayla. The race they did together was a disaster. The McGregor clan didn't do very well in competition today."

"Jade came in first."

"That's not surprising. She's my sports fanatic. How about Joshua?"

Annie rubbed her shoulder. "I'll recover, hopefully."

"What happened?"

"As you know, your youngest is very enthusiastic, and that carries over to his dancing."

"I volunteered to be his partner, but he wanted you. You've charmed your way into my children's lives. Mine, too."

Ian's compliment warmed her from the inside out. For a second Annie felt beautiful.

She just smiled. She'd better end this conversation before she kissed him on a playground full of hundreds of people. "See you at the end."

"Most definitely."

As Annie headed toward Jasmine, she felt relaxed. Talking with Ian was always easy, even when she'd told him about the fire. Sometimes she had to make herself remember he was her employer—like a moment ago—and that being with his children was a job that would end someday.

Annie approached Jasmine sitting on a blanket with a couple of her friends and an adult. Not far from her was Kayla with her mother and a group of girls. Jasmine had her back to Kayla, which was probably a good thing since the child was sending glares Jasmine's way. Annie settled next to her and greeted the others, who had all visited the house at different times.

"How are you doing, Jasmine?" Annie asked when she heard a remark from Kayla about how she'd tried to get a different partner for the race but the teacher wouldn't let her.

"Now that the race is over, fine. I tried to get Kayla to lock arms so we could work better together. She wouldn't, so we spent most of the time going back to the starting line when we lost our balloon." She spoke loud enough that Kayla would hear it.

Kayla gathered her girlfriends close and whispered something that caused them all to giggle and look toward Jasmine.

When Jasmine glared at Kayla, Annie laid a hand on the girl's shoulder. "Ignore her."

"I was here first, and she came and sat down with her friends. She did that on purpose to bug me."

"You're letting her control your behavior. Do you want her to have that kind of power?"

Jasmine clamped her lips together.

"Did you see her neck?" a girl behind Annie whispered loudly.

"Yeah, so gross."

Jasmine started to get up, her hands balled. "That's so rude."

Annie leaned close, keeping her in place. "I'm okay." Then she looked at Jasmine's friends. "What are you all going to do this summer?"

Everyone jumped in to answer. Jasmine settled down and said, "We have a pool Dad will open after Memorial Day, so you all can come and swim." That started the girls making plans for a swim party the first weekend in June.

Finally when Annie thought Jasmine was

okay, she rose. “I’m heading for Jeremy’s class. See you later.”

Giggles erupted from Kayla’s group. Annie slowed and glanced back. Suddenly she saw Jasmine launch herself at Kayla and wrestle her to the ground. Annie’s stomach clenched.

Chapter Eleven

Annie rushed forward at the same time Ian arrived and pulled his daughter off Kayla, while the girl's mother cried out, "She's hurting my baby!" The woman grabbed her daughter and smoothed her hair away from her face while Kayla sobbed.

"Dad, she said mean things about Annie." Jasmine's eyes shone with unshed tears, a scratch down her right cheek. "I couldn't let her get away with it."

"What did she say?" Ian asked, turning his attention from Kayla's dramatics.

Jasmine glanced at Annie then whispered something in Ian's ear. His expression darkened.

Annie didn't want the child getting in trouble because of her. "Jasmine, don't let Kayla—"

"She called you a monster. You aren't." Tears slipped down her cheeks.

Annie scanned the growing crowd and quashed the impulse to leave. She had to be here for Jasmine—and Ian. That was more important than how Kayla had insulted her. "I'm sorry she said that, but that doesn't mean you need to go after her. Please tell her you're sorry."

"I won't. She was wrong."

"But so were you." Annie saw Jasmine's teacher approaching. Mrs. Evans stopped and talked with Kayla and her mother first, then came over to Jasmine. "Kayla said you hit her for no reason."

"She said some things about Annie. Kayla's the ugly one."

"We don't tolerate fighting for any reason here, Jasmine. I think it's best if you go home with your dad, and I'll see you tomorrow morning in the principal's office before school. Then you can have your say."

When Mrs. Evans left, Jasmine sniffled and wiped away her tears. "I'm not sorry, Dad. Kayla had no right to make fun of Annie."

"We'll discuss this at home. Annie, will you walk with Jasmine while I get Joshua, Jeremy and Jade?"

"We'll be waiting at the car."

Annie and Jasmine walked in silence through the school hallways and out the front door. At the SUV Annie lounged against the hood, trying to figure out what to say to Jasmine.

"Do you think Dad's gonna ground me?"

"I can't say what your father is going to do, but I hope you'll apologize to Kayla for hitting her. Violence isn't the answer, Jasmine."

"She's a bully. She makes fun of people all the time and gets away with it. How can her mother sit there and let her do that?"

"Kayla and her mom aren't your concern. You can't control them. All you can control is your actions. If you can rise above what she does, others will see that. Girls like Kayla win when they get you in trouble."

"Aren't you mad about what she said?"

"I didn't hear it, and even if I had, I would have ignored it. She can't hurt me unless I let her." As she said those words, Annie realized she really believed them. "I can't make you say you're sorry, but forgiving Kayla will make you feel better. A person who makes fun of others and bullies them is someone who has problems. They are usually miserable. But God taught us to turn the other cheek."

Annie noticed Ian coming out of the school building with his other children. The sight of him brought forth that brief moment on the playground when they'd been talking.

Jeremy stopped near Jasmine. "Way to go, sis. I wish I could have seen it."

"Jeremy, get in the car, and the rest of you, too." Ian waited until his kids had piled inside the SUV then asked Annie, "Are you all right?"

"I'm more concerned about Jasmine. When I decided to wear the T-shirt, I knew something like that could happen. That's why I used to cover up my scars—explaining got tiresome. But today as I was talking to Joshua's friends about my scars, it didn't bother me like it used to."

"What should I say to Jasmine? I'd probably have said something to Kayla if I'd heard what she'd said. That girl is wrong, too."

"But you wouldn't have hit her." Annie turned to get into the car.

"You aren't going to tell me what you'd do in my place? I know you have an opinion."

"Ask Jasmine what she thinks should happen to her because of her actions. What should she have to do?"

Ian grinned. "Good idea."

After what happened at the picnic, no one spoke on the drive home. When Ian pulled into the garage, the children piled out and waited at the door to go inside.

"Zoe was always the one who disciplined the children," Ian explained. "I worked and she took care of the home. Then Aunt Louise took up where Zoe left off. Until my aunt died, I didn't have a lot of input into how the children acted. I didn't need to. They behaved, except for an occasional outburst. Jasmine and Jeremy have been so fragile lately. I don't want to make the situation worse."

"You'll do fine. The most important thing they need to know is that you love them and care about their problems. Children need love, consistency and stability."

"Not just children."

"True. Change is scary for anyone."

Ian opened his door and got out. Annie met him at the garage entrance to the breezeway. "I'll check on the others while you talk with Jasmine."

As she walked through the kitchen, she caught her reflection in the microwave door. Even in the vague image she could see the scars along her neck. Strange that what Kayla had said about her didn't hurt her. *There's more to me than my injury*, Annie thought, *and the people who count know it.* The smile Ian had given her when he'd seen her in the blue T-shirt told her that.

* * *

Ian made his way up the stairs. Jasmine usually retreated to her bedroom when she got in trouble. The door was closed, and he knocked on it.

"Go away!" she shouted from inside.

"Jasmine, we need to talk." Ian waited to see if she would open the door. When she did, he entered and took a seat on Jasmine's bed. His daughter stood in the middle of the room, hugging her arms to her chest and staring at the floor. "Why don't you sit, too?"

Jasmine remained where she was.

"You know, when I was a child, I got into a fight with a kid who used to call me the teacher's pet because I could answer all her questions. By that time I was one grade ahead of my age group and still pretty small. This boy was large."

Jasmine lifted her head. "Did he hurt you?"

"Yes, but I hurt him, too. All my anger welled up one day and exploded. The fight happened after school on the way home. He'd been teasing me all school year, and I'd had enough. I gave him a black eye and made his nose bleed. That's what stopped the fight. When I saw all that blood, I felt awful. The boy was on the ground, holding his nose and crying. Even at eleven I knew I wanted to help others rather than hurt them. I'd seen how my little brother had been hurt by kids picking on him because of his cleft palate.

"So I took off my shirt and gave it to him to stop the bleeding. At first he wouldn't take it. I sat with him and told him I was sorry."

Jasmine came to the bed and sat next to Ian. "But he hurt you first."

"Yes, but I hit him."

"Did he apologize?"

"No, but he left me alone after that."

"Did you get in trouble?"

"No, because no one saw the fight. My parents never found out until I told them."

Jasmine's eyes grew round. "You did? Why?"

"Because I felt guilty."

"You didn't start it."

"It takes two to fight. I participated. He made me do something I didn't want to do. I didn't like being controlled like that."

"Like Kayla did to me today?"

"Yes." Ian wound his arm around Jasmine's shoulder and pressed her to his side. "So what do you think I should do about you hitting Kayla?"

"I think I should be grounded until Monday."

"I agree. No friends over, no phone calls and no TV. Anything else?"

Jasmine shrugged. "I don't know."

Ian rose and looked down at his daughter. "Jasmine, if someone is bothering you, come and talk to me before it results in fighting. Keeping it inside doesn't solve anything."

As Ian left Jasmine's room, he wasn't sure he'd gotten his point across, but he felt optimistic. Usually Jasmine was anything but calm. Drama surrounded her life. But a few minutes ago he'd strengthened a bond with her that he hoped would help her think through her actions.

At the campground at Cimarron Lake on Memorial Day weekend, Ian and Jeremy finished putting up the girls' tent and stepped back to admire their work.

His eldest son grinned and said, "I'm glad we decided to come for Sunday night." He swiveled around and panned the people around them. "Boy, Annie has a big family, and she said not all of them are even here this weekend."

"Hi, I'm Nathan," a child about Jeremy's age said as he approached. "Uncle Ben always brings his dog with him, too."

"He does? What kind?" Jeremy glanced around.

"German shepherd. He's a service dog. At

least that's what Uncle Ben told us, but I don't know what Ringo does."

"This is my service dog. His name is Rex. I'm Jeremy."

"Do you want to meet my uncle? He's down at the lake, fishing."

Jeremy turned to Ian. "Can I, Dad?"

"Sure." He watched his son and Rex stroll with Annie's nephew toward the water.

"You've been abandoned already?"

He looked over his shoulder at Annie, her arms full of backpacks and bedding. "Yep, for another dog."

"That must be Ringo."

"Normally I would be concerned about a German shepherd, but I know how well Emma trains her animals."

"Ringo was her first service dog five years ago."

"What kind is Ringo?"

"There's a lot of research on how they help veterans who are suffering from PTSD. They can help with their panic attacks and anxiety."

Jeremy, Rex and Nathan disappeared down the slope to the lake. As he watched, Ian thought Annie's showing up in their lives had to be God's doing. He might never have thought about a service dog for his son, but Rex was just what his son needed. Jeremy was still moody, but he wasn't as angry. The doctor adjusted his medication, and it was finally working much better. That was progress.

"Where did the girls go? I thought they were helping you with our supplies."

Annie put down her load by the tent. "They put your stuff over there, but Carey came over and introduced herself. She's my ten-year-old niece. The girls hit it off and took Joshua to meet some of my younger nephews at the playground."

"Do you have much left?"

"One more trip should do it, then I'd like to check on Joshua. Usually one of the older nieces is watching the younger children. I want to let her know about Joshua and his tendency to get into trouble. By the way, does he swim? Since you have a pool, I was hoping so."

"You would think he was born in the water. He puts my other kids to shame."

After they carried the last of the gear to the tents, Ian walked with Annie toward the playground next to the area where the Knight family had set up camp.

"With so many children, you all got the best site to camp in," Ian remarked to Annie as he surveyed the ten tents of various sizes pitched for the group. "What's your secret? Memorial Day is usually crowded at spots like this in Oklahoma."

"My eldest brother and his family come a few days early."

"Let me see—that's Ken and his wife, Samantha. I need to carry a notepad around to keep everyone's name straight. I came from a small family. One brother who has a boy a little older than Jeremy. A couple of cousins and my mother. That's it."

"And they all live in South Carolina?"

"Yes. When Zoe died, I thought about moving back to be near them, but this is home for my kids. They didn't need any more disruption, and Aunt Louise came to help me."

Ian was amazed yet again how easy it was to talk to Annie. When he was in high school and met Zoe for the first time, he could barely say two sentences to her. "Would you believe I was once very shy?"

"You aren't now."

"That shy guy is still in me, but if I was going to date Zoe and if I was going to work with patients, I had to overcome it."

"How did you do it?"

"My wife. She wasn't shy. I guess I learned by necessity and her example. Zoe never met a stranger. Joshua takes after her."

Annie chuckled. "I guess we can do anything if properly motivated."

"Motivation is the key to change." Ian looked at the outskirts of the large playground filled with children. "How many belong to the Knight clan?"

"All but the three swinging over there." Annie pointed toward the far side of the area.

"That means minus my three, so there's twenty that I've seen."

"I told you I have a large family."

Ian smiled. "And I can tell how much you love your family, all gazillion of them."

"Well, not quite that many. Maybe minus a couple billion," Annie said with a straight face.

Laughter welled up in Ian. What a good start to the weekend. Especially after the past week of school with Jasmine suspended for two days before being allowed to go back Friday for the last day. "How did you get Jasmine to apologize to Kayla?"

"I talked to her several times about how much better she'd feel if she did. Sometimes the best way to deal with a bully is to be nice. To rise above her tactics."

Interesting that both he and Annie had given Jasmine basically the same message. More and more he felt they looked at life the same way.

"How did Kayla respond to Jasmine's apology for hitting her?"

"She got mad and stomped off."

"Odd."

"Not really. Kindness often highlights the other person's part in the incident. I'm hoping Kayla isn't feeling as though what she did is a victory." A gleam sparkled in Annie's eyes.

Ian inched closer and grazed his fingers down the side of her neck, the feel of scarred tissue nothing new to him. "In my work, I see them all the time. I'm used to them. I'm glad you don't feel as though you have to hide the scars from us."

"Why?"

"I want you to feel comfortable with us, like part of the family. And the fact that Jasmine listened to you says a great deal."

"Your children mean a lot to me, Ian."

And Annie meant a lot to him. Ian had one more doctor to contact and then he'd approach Annie with his plan. She'd done so much for him. He wanted to give back to her. In not quite two months, he had his family back. Ian wanted Annie to do what he was trying to do: put her past behind her.

"I'm going to the lake to check on Jeremy. Maybe do some fishing."

"I see Melissa supervising. I'm going to talk to her and then find my twin."

As Ian made his way toward the water, he felt a lightness in his steps. A couple of months ago he'd been dreading the summer months because his children were so unsettled, but now he wasn't. He owed Tom Hansen a gift for telling him about Annie.

The sunlight felt good when he stopped where Jeremy and Nathan were with Ben, who was putting bait on their fishing poles. A big smile on his son's face warmed him more than the sun.

"You must be Ben. I'm Ian. Annie's told me about you and your service dog." Ian shook the man's hand.

"As she has told me about Rex and what great things he's doing for Jeremy. My sister is excited that Rex is working out for you."

"He's the best dog." Jeremy moved toward a flat rock to fish next to Nathan.

"I came to see if you had an extra pole. I haven't gone fishing in years, but I understand the fish we catch will be tonight's meal."

Ben chuckled. "No pressure, huh?"

"You're kidding, aren't you? I'm sure there's a backup plan for dinner if we don't catch enough fish."

"Nope. We'll only have coleslaw and beans

if we don't get some. But others will be joining us here and down the shoreline."

"How come?"

"An incentive, so we will have enough fish to eat."

"Okay. Let me see if I remember what I know from being a child."

"The good thing is this lake is teeming with fish."

For two hours, Ian sat patiently on the bank, keeping his line in the water while everyone around him, even his son, caught fish after fish. Then when he was about to give up, he felt a tug on his line. Ian stood up, jerking the pole and hoping to set the hook in whatever he caught.

Jeremy pulled in his line. "I'll get the net. You can do this, Dad."

After the long wait Ian hoped for a big one, but instead he hauled in a white crappie that, according to Ben, weighed barely a pound. He'd envisioned a monster-size fish to make up for all the ones he didn't bring in. Good thing they weren't depending on him for supper.

Amanda came up behind him, whistling at the fish he passed to Ben. "I love crappie." She looked at the others that had been caught. "We're going to eat well tonight. Ian, I think they can do without you for a while. Can't you, Ben?"

"Sure. I'll keep an eye on Jeremy. He and Nathan are having fun."

"What's up?" Ian asked Amanda while glancing at his son, laughing with his new friend. The sound filled him with hope.

"Annie has a surprise for you. I'll show you. It's at the end of the Boomer Trail. Joshua has taken a shining to Melissa and is following her around with her little brother. Brent is six. We have a child or two around the ages of all of your children."

Ian strolled beside Amanda across the area where the Knight family tents were pitched and into the woods on a trail under a green canopy of trees, a light breeze ruffling their leaves.

"I need to get back," Amanda said. "I'm on the cooking detail tonight. I'm leaving you here. Keep on the trail." She pointed where to go. "It ends near a lake overlook. You'll see."

When Ian came to the end and the trail opened up onto a bluff that had a great view of the lake, he stopped and stared at the blanket spread over the ground with a picnic basket in one corner. He walked to the wicker container and lifted the top. Inside was a bottle of sparkling grape juice and two glasses set between bowls of large strawberries and melted chocolate.

He heard a branch snap and looked up. Annie

rounded the last bend in the trail. When she saw him, she looked puzzled. She gazed at the basket and blanket, and her expression went blank.

"What's this?" She paused on the opposite side of the coverlet.

"You tell me."

"I can't."

"Your sister said that you wanted to see me."

Annie's eyes brightened with understanding quickly followed by irritation. "Jasmine told me that you wanted to see *me*. I thought this was a strange place to meet."

"Why?"

"Because the locals call this bluff Lover's Leap." Annie averted her eyes to the lake stretching out below. "You know what's going on here?"

Jasmine? Ah, now he did. "How did my daughter rope your sister into participating in this little…" He waved his arm, at a loss for words.

"Rendezvous." Annie's cheeks flamed.

"Yes."

"Amanda is a romantic. It wouldn't have taken much. Now I know for sure who was leaving those little gifts for me. I suspected one of them, but I think it was both!"

"True—if one does something like this, then

the other is involved, too." Ian removed the sparkling grape juice from the basket, then the strawberries and chocolate. He chuckled. "They've been watching too much TV."

"No, my sister is a huge romance reader. This is all her. The girls probably came up with the idea of doing something, and Amanda went to town with it."

Ian sat on the blanket. "We might as well enjoy it. I love strawberries and chocolate, not that I've ever had them together."

"I do, too, which Amanda would know."

"But sparkling grape juice?"

"We have this every year on New Year's Eve. We like the bubbles." Annie sat down on the other side of the blanket.

"With your large family, you must have a lot of traditions, especially during a holiday like this one." Ian opened the bottle and poured the grape juice into two glasses, then passed one to Annie. He'd have to thank Amanda and Jasmine. This was a good idea.

"Just wait until the Fourth. My brothers revert back to childhood with their fireworks display."

Ian raised his drink. "To the next holiday."

"Father's Day. Just a few weeks away. So what do you do to celebrate?"

"Usually we go to the Oklahoma City Zoo

for the day. If it's raining, we spend the day inside at the Omniplex next to the zoo."

"No golfing or sleeping in a hammock?" Annie dipped the first strawberry into the chocolate and took a bite.

"I've never played golf and don't own a hammock, although it wouldn't be a bad idea to get one."

Annie fixed another strawberry and held it out for Ian. "So what are we going to do about my sister and your daughters?"

Ian leaned toward her hand and sank his teeth into the juicy fruit. "How about nothing? I'm enjoying this quiet alone time with good food and drink." He scanned the woods surrounding the bluff and whispered, "I wouldn't be surprised if one or all are watching right now. Want to find out?"

"How?"

"I can't imagine my daughters remaining quiet if I kiss you."

Annie's eyes grew round. "You're probably right."

"Feed me another strawberry, and then I'll thank you with a kiss."

"Do you think we should encourage them by doing that?"

"True. No telling what they would plan." But the idea of kissing Annie again wouldn't leave

Ian's mind. In fact, he'd often recalled that kiss on his patio. "But it might be fun finding out what they would do."

Annie laughed and picked up a strawberry, dipped it in some chocolate then presented it to Ian. "If I didn't know better, I'd think you wanted to kiss me anyway."

Ian ignored the offered fruit and bent closer to her. "Actually, I do."

A small gasp escaped her beautiful lips, but she didn't pull back. Instead, she leaned toward him.

Suddenly Jade entered the clearing, shouting, "Dad, come quick!"

Chapter Twelve

"What's going on?" Ian shot to his feet.

"Is Jeremy having a seizure?" Annie jumped up.

Jade shook her head. "Joshua's missing."

The three started hurrying down the trail back to the campground. "How?" Annie asked. "Melissa is always so conscientious."

"We were playing hide-and-seek, and we can't find him."

"Where?" Ian asked.

"Around the playground." Jade looked panicked.

Annie increased her pace to keep up with Ian. "We'll find him. There are a lot of us." But she kept thinking of Joshua's adventurous behavior. He'd try anything he thought would be fun. There were some caves not too far from where they were camping. What if he got lost in one or encountered a bear? Her own fear skyrocketed as risky scenarios ran through her mind.

Slightly behind Annie on her right, Jade said, "Melissa didn't do anything wrong. Don't blame her."

Annie slowed and glanced back at Jade. "I'm not putting blame on anyone. I just want to find Joshua." As her heartbeat raced she accelerated, nearly catching up with Ian. In the distance she heard Joshua's name being called, which confirmed he was still missing.

A few minutes later, Ian burst out of the woods first and headed straight for a group of adults, including Melissa and Annie's father, gathered near the playground. "Where have you looked?" Ian scanned their faces, his shoulders slumping.

Annie touched his arm as she parked herself next to him. "Dad?"

"Ken and Charlie are checking the caves. Ben and some of the older kids are walking along the shoreline."

"I've looked in all the hiding places the children were using," Melissa said, her face pale and her hands shaking.

Annie crossed to her niece and clasped her hands. "This isn't your fault. Things happen that we would never anticipate. And to Joshua especially. How long has he been missing?"

"Fifteen minutes."

Annie's eldest sister, Rachel, pointed to the left. "We've tried all the tents and cars. That leaves the woods. We need to look there, too."

Annie's dad started organizing the family. "Let's form a line with four or five feet between each of us and comb them."

Ian approached Melissa. "Joshua has gotten away from me before. He usually follows directions, but something might get into his head and he forgets what he should do. Don't feel responsible for this."

Tears welled in the teenager's eyes. "He'd been doing everything I said."

Rachel, Melissa's mother, joined them and hugged her daughter. "The best thing to do is help find him, so come on."

While Amanda stayed back at camp in case Joshua returned on his own, Annie said to Ian, "Let's go toward the trail. Maybe he saw us and decided to follow."

"But we were just there."

"He might have cut through the woods at an angle. Joshua looks at everything as an escapade."

"That's something he would do," Ian agreed. He pushed his way through some thick underbrush at the edge of the forest, shouting his son's name.

Annie did likewise about five feet from Ian. As they neared the bluff, Annie thought she heard a voice say, "I'm here!" Halting, she waved to Ian and put her forefinger to her mouth. He stopped yelling Joshua's name.

"Help. I'm stuck!"

The sound came from the area in front of Annie. She hastened forward with Ian running toward her. "Joshua, where are you?"

"Here. In the log."

Up ahead Annie spied a large log, and it appeared one end was hollow. An animal like a fox could fit in it, but a child?

"We're coming, Joshua," Ian shouted.

"I'm here." When Annie reached the log a few seconds before Ian, she knelt at one end of the downed tree trunk and peeked inside.

"I can't move." Annie saw Joshua's legs wiggle as though trying to back out of the log.

Ian went to the other end and peered in. He grinned. "You've got yourself in a pickle, son."

"A pickle? I wish I had one to eat. I'm hungry."

"It means you're in a tight spot."

"Yeah, Dad. That's what I said."

Annie squatted next to Ian, the sight of Joshua's dirty face wonderful. "We could try to pull him out."

"Where are your arms?"

"At my sides."

Ian stood and walked around the six-foot log, knocking against the wood, checking for soft spots. The raps echoed through the woods.

"It's narrower at the end where his head and torso are. We should try pulling him out by the legs." He returned to the other end of the log. "I'll tug on your legs, but you'll have to let us know if you're caught on anything. Annie will stay here and talk to you." He stooped and whispered in her ear, "The wood is rough so it'll probably scrape his arms. Reassure him while I try to dislodge him."

Annie lay on the ground facing Joshua and reached in to touch his head. "I'm staying here while your dad gets you out. What made you hide in here?"

"Cuz I was being found. I wanna fool everyone."

"It fooled them so well they thought you were lost."

"I'm not lost. I know where I am." He giggled. "That means I won."

Ian pulled on Joshua's legs. The boy moved slightly, wincing.

"Does it hurt?"

He wiggled and managed to bring one arm out from under his body. “I’m tough.”

“I know you’re tough, buddy.” Annie peered over the log at Ian.

He continued to pull. When Joshua suddenly popped loose, Ian’s furrowed forehead and set jaw quickly relaxed.

Annie hurried to Ian as Joshua slid out. She wanted to scoop the child into her arms, but Ian did first.

“Don’t ever scare me like that again, Joshua. I had visions of having to saw you out of the log.” Ian held the boy away from him and checked his arms and body for any wounds. “When we get back to camp, I need to clean these scrapes on your arms, but other than those you seem fine.”

Joshua threw his arms around Ian’s neck. “Thanks, Dad. You saved me.”

Ian grinned from ear to ear as he rose with his son in his arms.

Annie patted Joshua’s back. “No more hide-and-seek. In fact, I’m not sure you’ll leave my side the rest of the weekend.”

“Aw. I was supposed to hide. It was a cool place. I didn’t know I’d get stuck.”

Ian set Joshua on the ground and tousled his hair. “Annie is right. You have to be within view of one of us the rest of the weekend. Trouble seems to find you."

Joshua lifted his shoulders. "I don't look for trouble. Promise."

"C'mon. We need to get back and let my family know you've been located." Annie started toward camp with the five-year-old between her and Ian.

"Now that the kids have gone to sleep, do you want to share the strawberries and chocolate? The grape juice is flat but that's okay." Ian was carrying the picnic basket and sat in the folding chair next to Annie on one side of the fire circle while her sister and Ben sat across from them.

Annie's first impulse was to say no because of how close she and Ian had come to kissing again. But she'd enjoyed the snacks and with her sister and brother-in-law nearby, there wouldn't be a repeat of what Ian had suggested at the bluff. Annie always thought of herself as being strong willed, but Ian was testing that assumption.

"Sure. I hate my sister having gone to all this trouble to set this up and not at least have the treats." She'd raised her voice so Amanda would hear her reply.

Annie slanted a glance toward Amanda and

Ben exchanging whispers. Probably plotting something for her and Ian tomorrow. With all that had happened concerning Joshua and then dinner and cleanup, Annie hadn't had the time to tell her sister to stop interfering. Amanda had tried it once before, and Annie had thought she'd made her wishes very clear: no trying to fix her up.

"I think my sister was behind it all and somehow solicited your daughters to help," Annie whispered to Ian.

"Did you say anything to the girls when you said good-night?" Ian dipped a strawberry into the chocolate and passed it to Annie, their fingers touching.

Annie tried to concentrate, but all she could think about was their almost kiss on the bluff. She had to admit it: she'd wanted Ian to kiss her.

"Annie?"

She blinked and peered at him. "Yes. Jasmine and Jade looked at each other, struggling to keep straight faces, and said that my sister asked them to help her set it up today, then they burst out giggling."

Annie popped the piece of fruit into her mouth then licked the chocolate off her fingertips, trying not to think of when she'd fed the strawberry to Ian.

"Which means they are guilty."

"I'm not really mad at them, but at my sister, who is encouraging them. She knows better."

"She wants to see you with someone."

Annie huffed and glared at Amanda. "Being with someone isn't in my plan." But even as she said it, it didn't feel right. That bothered her even more. Once it had been her dream to have a husband and children.

"What plan?"

"Working with children who need me is my plan. I'm not looking for anything else." If she said it enough, maybe she would believe it.

"How about a man who needs you?"

Ian's question hung in the air. Annie averted her gaze and watched Amanda and Ben get up and walk toward their tent, Ben's arm resting on her sister's shoulder. A pang zipped through Annie at the sight. She'd wanted that at one time.

She didn't know how to answer Ian. He wasn't aware of her part in the fire. If he knew the truth, would he still want her? "What man?" she finally asked.

"Me. Do you not see how important you are to me and my family? You have given me hope for the future. Hope that my children will be all right. That I'll be okay."

"I understand. You're grateful for what I'm

doing." Annie stood. "I appreciate that. I like being needed." Because it eased the pain of her guilt for a short time. "I'm going to turn in now."

Ian caught her hand. "Annie, don't go yet. Please stay."

Annie studied his face, highlighted by the dying fire. He was such a good man. She cared for him more than she should. But—

"Please, Annie. Our one time of quiet was interrupted today."

She sat again, although now she realized how close they were. Only inches separated them.

"Do you realize how extraordinary you are?"

"What am I supposed to say to that? Yes, I am? No, I'm not?"

"I should have said instead that you're a special person, period. No question about it. I think you sell yourself short."

Annie turned her folding chair so she could face him and put some space between them. "I know I can help children. I'm not afraid of difficult cases."

"That's not what I'm saying. When you first came to us, you kept your scars a secret, hiding them. I'm not sure you would have shared them with us if it hadn't been for Jeremy. I'm glad you did, but it doesn't change how I look at you or how I feel about you."

"They're a reminder of what I did." Annie dropped her gaze to her lap. She was going to tell him. Outside her family and a few firefighters, no one knew. And she didn't talk about it, even with Amanda, the person closest to her. But Ian deserved to know, and if it made a difference, so be it.

"A reminder of what? The fire? Why would you want to do that? That's the past. What's done is done."

Annie took a deep breath and held it for a long moment before slowly exhaling. The knots of tension in her stomach remained. "Ian, I'm responsible for the fire. I didn't…" She couldn't say it.

He leaned forward in his chair, resting his elbows on his thighs. "What happened?"

Annie swallowed several times, but she felt as if a fist was jammed in her throat. Tears sprang to her eyes, and she looked toward her tent. She wanted to escape. She shouldn't have stayed. She shouldn't have started this conversation.

Ian reached out and took her hand. "Please tell me, Annie."

She tugged her hand free. "I lit a candle on the table by the open window in my bedroom at the cabin. I was there with part of my family. Usually Amanda and I share a bedroom, but she didn't come that weekend. I thank God for that at least. I fell asleep on my bed and didn't blow out the candle. The curtains…" A vision of the flames licking up the walls when she woke up coughing still haunted her. "They caught fire, and the dry timber of the walls quickly went up in the blaze. My father rescued me but couldn't get back in to help my mom. She became trapped like I did. She died because of me." Annie rushed the last sentence.

Ian moved from his chair and knelt in front of her. "Annie, it was an accident." He clasped her arms and waited until she looked at him.

Through tears she saw his dear face so full of concern and compassion. "An accident I caused. If only I hadn't…" She couldn't say what she had agonized over for fourteen years.

"Hadn't lit the candle? I've dealt with many patients who have done things they regretted, things that led to bad consequences. Some did them on purpose and others accidentally. The latter are the people who have the most problems dealing with their guilt."

"Of course I feel guilt. My mother died because of me. How do you get over that?"

"By turning to the Lord. I know He's forgiven you. Now you need to do the same thing for yourself. Let the past go."

Annie shot to her feet, tipping over the folding chair, and yanked away from Ian. "It's not that easy."

He rose. "I didn't say it was. Does your family blame you?"

She shook her head.

"So the only one who does is you?"

"Because *I did it.*" The words tore from deep inside her.

"You saw with Jeremy what happens when you keep feelings locked away. They eat at you, grow bigger in your mind. God doesn't want that for you."

Annie stepped back, nearly tripping over the downed chair. "You don't know what God wants for me."

"Do you? Are you doing His will or yours?"

"You don't understand. My scars are my…" Annie couldn't get a decent breath. Her throat burned. Her chest tightened.

Ian closed the space between them. "Punishment? I don't see that being the Lord's plan for you. He gave you a beautiful gift for working with children. You didn't cause that fire with malicious intent. When are you going to feel you've paid enough?"

"Why are you doing this?"

"Because I care for you. I lo—" His eyes widened, and he moved back.

Anger swelled in Annie. Not even Amanda

had pushed her this much. "What, loathe? Like? Maybe you pity me."

Ian's gaze drilled into her. "I'm falling in love with you."

"The only feeling you have for me is gratitude for my help. Don't confuse that with anything more." Annie swept around and marched toward her tent.

At the opening she paused, trying to calm her trembling. She squeezed her hands into a ball. She didn't want the girls to know anything had happened. Why couldn't Ian let things alone? Let her work for him and care for his children?

Just for a second her heart had leaped when he'd said the word *love.* Now she didn't know how long she could stay at the McGregors'. By the age of twenty she'd realized love wasn't in her future. Not after David.

Ian wasn't David... But still, Annie couldn't risk being hurt anymore.

Ian wanted to go after her, but he knew she would reject him. Yes, he was grateful that Annie was in their lives, but it was much more than that. Up until a few minutes ago he hadn't realized how much. There was a lot to love about Annie.

Why doesn't she see the beauty I do?

Her guilt was robbing her of the life she

should have had. Ian wasn't going to give up helping her see that, or the medical fact that there were procedures that would make her scars less noticeable, especially her ear. Ian knew that until she accepted that what happened was an accident, she'd never be free of the past. Every day when Annie looked at herself those scars reminded her of her mom's death.

Maybe he could solicit Amanda and her family to help convince her to have surgery, especially if it didn't cost her anything. Ian wanted to give her that chance to heal.

"Thanks for coming to help me," Ian said a few days later to Amanda, whom he'd invited to help chaperone Jeremy's belated-birthday swimming party.

"Someone has to shake some sense into Annie. I've been trying. Dad has. Even my youngest brother. She won't listen. I think she's gotten so used to feeling that guilt she's afraid to let go of it. She and our mother were very close, probably closer than any of us were. But I know Mom would be so upset if she knew what Annie is doing."

Ian greeted Ben, who was coming up the steps to the porch. "I'm glad you've been a lifeguard before." Ian shook Annie's brother-in-law's hand. "I probably let Jeremy invite too many, but I was thrilled he wanted to. I couldn't say no when he kept adding boys to the list."

"Are your other children going to be here?" Ben asked.

"Yes, they invited a couple of friends, too."

Amanda laughed. "Good thing they aren't a little older or there might be problems. Four girls at a party with eight boys."

"Please don't remind me about what I'll be dealing with in a few years," Ian said with a chuckle.

"You hope it takes that long," Amanda said as she headed for the kitchen to help Annie with the food.

"Amanda told me about what you were going to do later." Ben crossed the foyer toward the hallway with Ian.

"It's my version of an intervention. No matter what she feels about me, I want her to do this for herself."

"Have the surgery or forgive herself?"

Ian opened the sliding glass door to the patio. "Let the past go. Ben, I just noticed you don't have your dog with you."

"No, I want to focus totally on the children in the water. Besides, this is Jeremy and Rex's show. I want all the attention on them. Ringo can be an attention hog at times."

"By the way, my children, even Joshua with his scrapes, had a great time last week with all the others."

"I understand Nathan is coming to the party."

"Yes, Jeremy and Nathan hit it off that day fishing. I also had Annie invite her niece Carey because Jasmine and Jade really enjoyed themselves with her."

"Where are your kids?"

"Cleaning up outside. Annie has everyone working, even Joshua." The front doorbell rang. "I've got to get this."

"I'll supervise the preparation for the party."

Ian answered the door and let in a steady stream of children while telling the parents when to pick them up. After everyone arrived, he headed for the kitchen to let Annie and Amanda know the party was starting. As he approached the room, he overheard Annie saying, "I'm not going to say anything until I've found someone."

Ian walked through the doorway. "Found someone for what?"

At the sink Annie whirled around and stared at him, her expression stamped with surprise.

"Excuse me. I'm going to help my husband with the children out back." Amanda hurried from the house.

Silence hung between Annie and Ian. His mouth went dry. Something was wrong.

"Is there a problem I should know about?"

"I'm looking for a replacement for me as your nanny."

Chapter Thirteen

The shock on Ian's face made Annie want to snatch the words back.

Ian opened his mouth to say something, shook his head and pivoted. The sound of the back door slamming reverberated through the kitchen. Her body trembling, Annie collapsed against the counter behind her, her stomach roiling. After coming home from the camping trip with her family last weekend, she'd realized she couldn't work for Ian any longer. He threatened everything she had planned for herself. He wasn't really falling in love with her, and he'd realize that and break her heart. Ian was grateful for her help and only said that because he took pity on her. She'd had enough of that the past fourteen years.

Annie couldn't stay here. Ian would see the wisdom when she found him a good nanny to replace her. Annie would stay until she did. She cared far too much for him to let a relationship based on false assumptions go anywhere.

Annie began taking the food outside. After setting up all the treats for the party, she scanned the children, glad to see so many attending. Several hung around Jeremy and Rex on one side of the pool while the girls remained across from them, giggling and occasionally pointing at the boys. The only ones in the water were Joshua and Brent, Annie's nephew. Once she'd seen Joshua at the lake swimming, she felt more at ease with him in the water. He was a good swimmer for his age.

Then her gaze fell on Ian at the other end of the pool with Ben. A frown carved deep lines into Ian's face. His stiff stance screamed his anger. At her.

Amanda approached her. "Are you all right?"

"No. That was not the way I was going to tell him. I didn't even want to say anything until I had a good lead on a nanny."

"If you really want to leave, he has a right to know from the beginning."

"I guess." But what if he fired her right after the party? Annie wasn't ready to go yet. She hadn't even talked with the children about it.

Make up your mind. You can't have it both ways.

Amanda turned toward her and lowered her voice. "My problem is why you think you need to leave. He's a great catch and you love all his children. This could be the family you've always wanted."

"Being a nanny has satisfied my need."

"Has it really? When we were kids all you talked about was having a family like the one we had."

"Whose side are you on?"

"Always yours, even when I think you're wrong. But that doesn't mean I won't try to straighten you out."

"What if Ian is interested in me because of his children? In fact, that makes the most sense."

"Why are you selling yourself short?" Amanda asked in a furious whisper.

"I'm being realistic. I see myself in the mirror. And Ian hasn't even seen the worst of my scars."

"He's a plastic surgeon. He knows what burn scars look like."

Joshua swam to the steps and exited the water, then walked quickly to Annie. "See, I'm not running." The child grinned.

"Walk any faster and you are. You love pushing the limits." Annie smiled and brushed his blond curls off his forehead.

"No one but me and Brent are swimming. Come in the water, Annie."

Although she'd grown up loving to swim like Joshua, she hadn't planned to go into the pool. Annie wore a one-piece swimsuit under a long T-shirt just in case she needed to help a child in the water, but she didn't wear her suit other than with her family.

When she didn't say anything, Joshua tugged on her hand. At first she resisted, then when all eyes were on her, she gave up and followed, intending only to sit on the top step. When she did, Joshua did a cannonball right next to her, totally drenching her.

"You're wet now. You might as well come in." Joshua swam toward her.

Annie waited until he was within arm's reach and grabbed him. After twirling him around, she playfully heaved him away from her.

When he surfaced, his giggles erupted, and he came toward her again. Annie slipped into the water and stood her ground until he was right on her, then darted away. He tried to catch her. "Come and get me," she taunted Joshua, her laughter filling the air.

He swam as fast as he could, and this time she let him get her, launching himself at her and taking them both under the water. When Annie and Joshua popped to the surface, the boys started jumping into the pool, seeing who could make the biggest splash. She glanced toward Ian and Ben, who were now both soaking wet.

As she started to look away, Ian's gaze riveted her. Even from a distance she could see his green eyes darkening to a brewing storm. Annie shivered. When he joined the boys in the water, she swam to the steps and hurried out of the pool, making sure her shirt covered most of her scars. To hide what was left of her right ear, she donned a floppy sunhat, then wrapped herself in a beach towel she'd placed nearby.

As the girls dived into the water, Amanda sidled up next to Annie. "You were having fun. Have you thought about how much you're going to miss that?"

"Thank you for that observation."

"Were you aware a couple of times the damage to your ear was visible, and Joshua didn't react to it? In fact, no one did."

"Why are you pushing me so hard?"

"Because I don't want you to make the biggest mistake of your life."

"I already did that the night I lit that candle."

When Amanda murmured, "You don't have to be that way," Annie began walking away.

Annie wanted to throttle her twin. She'd always counted on Amanda's support and needed it to do what she must. Because deep inside, she didn't know how she was going to deal with leaving this family she loved.

Something was up with Amanda and Ian. They had been talking together for the past ten minutes and from the looks of it, arguing. All the guests had left a half an hour ago except her sister and Ben. The surprise was when her eldest brother, who was Brent's father, had invited Joshua to spend the night when he'd come to pick up her nephew. Annie helped Joshua pack. He was so excited about his first sleepover.

She checked on the twins and Jeremy, camped out in the den with Ben watching a movie. The kitchen, poolside and yard were clean, so she decided to go to her apartment and collapse. When Ian had insisted she take the rest of the night off, she hadn't turned down the offer. Today had been fun, nerve racking and draining. Ian could see her sister and brother-in-law out.

In her apartment, Annie sank onto the couch and lay down, cushioning her head on a pillow. She needed to come up with a nanny for the children. At the moment she couldn't think of anyone—everyone had a job already. And Ian's kids needed someone who was special, patient, loving and…

Her eyelids slid closed, her exhaustion catching up with her.

When a loud knock at the door woke her, Annie bolted up on the couch. She wanted to pretend she wasn't in her apartment.

Another knock sounded and Amanda said, "I know you're in there. I'm not leaving." When Annie opened the door, Ian stood behind Amanda. Annie took one look at both of them and tried to shut the door.

Amanda blocked it with her body. "I told you I wasn't leaving. I could have invited the rest of the family, but I didn't. They think everything is okay."

Annie backed away. "It is." Then to Ian she added, "Why are you here?"

"Actually, I'm the one who wanted to talk to you. Amanda insisted on coming, too. It's hard to say no to your sister."

"Tell me about it. You two might as well come in and have your say. Then you can leave. It's been a long day." *And will probably be a longer night.*

Annie took a chair set across from the couch where they sat. "Ian, I'm sorry you had to find out about my leaving that way."

"That's not why I'm here. I'd planned on talking to you tonight even before I knew that."

"Then, what do you want to say?"

Ian sat forward on the couch, his hands loosely clasped. "I contacted a good friend I went to medical school with. He lives in Dallas and is a plastic surgeon, too. He's agreed to see you and assess your situation."

"I can't afford it."

"Free of charge. I've made all the arrangements. Everyone will be donating their services, so you won't have to worry about how much it is. He thinks a prosthetic ear will probably be the best way to go. He can see you next week. I'll drive you down."

Annie gripped the arms of the chair. "Do I have a say in this?"

"Yes, but you have no reason to say no now. I've taken care of the financial issue."

"And you still want to do this even though I'll be leaving you when a new nanny is found?"

"Yes." She saw a twitch in his jaw.

Do you think I'm that repulsive? Annie almost asked. She bit the inside of her cheek to keep the words to herself. "What about the children?"

"Dad will take care of them that day. His summer-school teaching job won't start for another two weeks," Amanda said.

"I see. You two worked this out without asking me if I would even go to the appointment."

They both nodded, solemn expressions on their faces.

Annie didn't know what she felt. She guessed she could go and at least hear out Ian's friend. She'd been half-afraid when he'd come into the apartment he was going to ask her to leave immediately—he'd been so angry at her today. He'd spoken to her only when absolutely necessary.

"Okay I'll go—on one condition. Ian, I won't leave until you find someone the children will love. That's the least I can do whether or not I agree to have surgery."

Ian stared right through her as though she wasn't sitting a few feet from him. "You'll have the job as long as you want. And believe me, I'll keep my distance and my feelings to myself," he said icily. He rose. "As you said, it's been a long day. Good night."

The sound of his footsteps resonated through her place as he made his way to the door. The last look of disappointment in his eyes nearly undid Annie. But she wasn't the right person for him. She was damaged, and when she left, he would realize that his feelings weren't based on love but gratitude.

"Do you know anyone who could be their nanny?" Annie asked Amanda, suddenly feeling as though she'd let everyone down. But Ian needed to realize what he thought he was feeling toward her could probably be extended to anyone who did a good job with his children.

"Actually I do. She just graduated from high school last year and went to Oklahoma State her freshman year, but she has decided to attend Cimarron Community College in the fall. Mary is great with children. I think she could work her school schedule around the children's in the fall. She wants to be a teacher, but OSU was too big for her. She wants the feel of a small college."

"Mary Franklin? That tall, redheaded beauty with men lined up at her front door during school holidays?"

"Yes. I could talk to her and let you know if she's interested. When she was in high school, she worked as a nanny for the Grimms across the street when their three children were out for summer break."

"I guess you can check with her." This was the answer to Annie's problem, yet she couldn't put any enthusiasm into the sentence.

"I thought you would be excited that I knew someone. Are you having second thoughts about leaving?"

"Of course not." But Annie sounded weak even to herself.

Amanda hugged Annie. "Good. You're having doubts about what you think you need to do. These past couple of months I've seen you changing. You're more open. You've shared with Ian and his children more of yourself than you have with anyone else. That includes your own family members."

"But he wants me to have surgery as if I'm not good enough this way." Annie swept her arm down her length.

"That's not what he's doing, and I think in your heart you know that. Ian wants you to have options and to make your own decision. He took the money factor away so you could look into your heart and decide what *you* want."

Annie straightened, thrusting back her shoulders. "It's my life. People should accept me as is."

"Yes. And in a perfect world, they would. Sometimes people react before thinking."

Mentally exhausted, Annie tried to stifle a yawn but couldn't.

"There's no use talking about the surgery until you hear what the doctor says. You're tired. Go to bed. I'll let myself out."

Annie switched off the lamp and walked toward the light streaming from her bedroom. But even after she got ready for bed and lay down, she couldn't quiet her thoughts, all centered on Ian. Even if she let herself love, Ian was used to making people as close to perfect as he could. And she would never be that.

"You've been awfully quiet on the ride back. Do you have any questions you didn't ask Neil?" Ian glanced at Annie sitting in the passenger seat of his Lexus.

"Dr. Hawks was quite thorough. I have all the information I need."

"What do you think?"

"I don't know. It's happened so fast, and the fact he can do the surgery next month makes me feel rushed."

Ian gritted his teeth. He'd hoped Annie would be excited once she heard from Neil what could be done to improve her scars and replace her ear. She'd helped his family so much—why couldn't she see that and accept the gift for what it was, a thank-you?

"The choice is yours, of course."

"Then, why did you arrange this?"

Ian gripped the steering wheel tighter. "Because you'd said you couldn't afford it, and I wanted at least to take that barrier out of the decision."

It had been nearly a week since Jeremy's swim party, when Annie's news about leaving had rocked his world, and he still hadn't been able to right it. She wanted to quit. Ian was trying to keep his developing feelings for her to himself, but it was hard when all he wanted to do was hold her and make her life better. To love her as she deserved. He might never have considered a service dog for Jeremy if she hadn't suggested the possibility. Rex was the best thing that had happened to his son.

"My life is fine the way it is."

The defensive tone in her voice made Ian wonder if she was trying to convince herself. "Are you sure you feel that way?"

"I should know how I feel."

"Your words don't match your tone."

Annie folded her arms over her chest and stared out her window.

Fifteen minutes later, Ian exited I-35 onto I-40, not far from Cimarron City. The closer they got to home, the more the tension thickened in the car.

"I don't want you to leave." Ian had to try one more time.

Annie didn't respond.

No one could replace Annie. Disappointment, anger and a deep hurt mingled inside him. "I haven't told the kids. I don't want to until the plans are firm."

"I won't tell them. But I have a lead on a good applicant."

Oh, joy. Ian had been hoping Annie couldn't

find anyone. Maybe this applicant wouldn't be acceptable. "Annie, I have feelings for you that have nothing to do with gratitude."

"How do you know that?"

"And how do you know they are? To quote you, I should know how I feel."

"Touché." Annie sat forward. "I see the exit to Cimarron City. We should be at your house shortly. I'll talk with Mary Franklin today and set up a time for you to interview her."

"I won't interview her at the house. If she doesn't work out—" and he was sure she wouldn't "—I don't want the children upset unnecessarily."

"How about I take the kids to Sooner Park? They love going there. According to Jasmine the playground is 'to die for.'"

"Your leaving won't change what I feel for you. I know you feel something for me. We work well together as a team."

"Yes, employee and employer."

"You're scared to really feel. Be honest with yourself and me. Annie, do you care about me beyond being your employer?"

Again she stared out the window. Ian didn't know if she would answer him.

"Yes," she finally said. "But I have my life figured out. I know what I'm supposed to do."

"What?"

"As I told you before, help children in need. My mother was the best there was. I'm continuing her work."

"How?"

"My parents used to take in foster children, and Mom especially would be the kids' support until a home was found for them. Being single, I can't easily take in foster children, so I chose to work with families whose children needed something extra."

"Like mine," Ian murmured.

"Yes."

"They still need you."

"But you're doing great with them, and with the right nanny you all will be fine."

"Can you guarantee that?" Sarcasm edged his voice, frustration churning his gut. After Ian pulled into his driveway and parked in the garage, he turned toward her. "What if everything you've started falls apart? You aren't your mother. You are Annie Knight. God has His own plan for you."

"Don't you get it? I'm the reason my mother isn't alive. I'm filling her void. Then maybe..." She pressed her lips together and unbuckled her seat belt.

"You can't forgive yourself for your mother's death. But her path isn't yours. The Lord has a unique plan for each person."

Annie shoved open the door and scrambled out of the Lexus, then leaned down, glaring. "Who are you to tell me what's best for me?"

"A guy who wants a great life for you, who loves you." Ian finally said aloud what he'd known in his heart for days. He wasn't just falling in love. He'd loved Annie Knight for a long time now. She'd been a breath of fresh air in a very stale life.

Her eyes grew big. She straightened, closed the passenger door and hurried toward the breezeway into the house.

Ian slammed his palm against the steering wheel. His love hadn't made any difference.

Chapter Fourteen

Annie couldn't get away from Ian fast enough. He was delusional to think he was in love with her. And yet, when he had said it, her heart had soared—until she'd forced reality into the situation.

Annie found her father coming into the McGregors' kitchen as she entered the house.

"The doctor couldn't help you?" he asked, covering the distance between them.

"No, actually, he could."

"Why the sad face, then?" Her dad glanced over her left shoulder.

Although Annie hadn't heard Ian enter, she knew he was behind her. "Lots of decisions to make. Are the children in bed yet?"

"I just said good-night to Joshua. The girls are playing a game, and Jeremy and Rex are watching TV. I think Rex is more into the show than Jeremy."

Annie walked to her father and kissed him on the cheek. "Thanks for helping today. I'm going to say good-night to Joshua and check in with the others before I go to my apartment."

Annie didn't even know how she strung words together to form coherent sentences, but she did. The closer Ian came to her in the kitchen, the faster her heart beat. She had to get out of there before she actually believed he could love her.

Ian had so much to offer the right woman. But Annie wasn't that person.

Upstairs she eased open Joshua's door to see if he was asleep. There was a hump in the middle of his bed with a light shining through the sheet. She tiptoed to his bed and began tickling him. "Boo! A certain little boy hasn't gone to sleep like he was supposed to."

Giggles floated from behind the blue sheet, then Joshua popped up and Daisy shot off the bed and raced out of the room.

"What were you doing?" Annie said in a stern voice while trying not to laugh.

"Trying to sneak Daisy in here." Joshua grinned. "We were hiding, but she doesn't like the dark. I got the flashlight."

"I think the only one around here who doesn't like the dark is you." Annie sat on the edge of his bed. "And you know it's Jade's turn for Daisy to sleep with her."

"Shh. She doesn't know I sneaked into her room and got Daisy."

At that moment Jade stomped into Joshua's room, carrying Daisy. "I did, too. What goes around comes around." Then she spun about on her heel and left with the dog.

He scrunched up his nose. "What's that mean?"

"One day she's going to take Daisy from you when it's your night to have the dog."

"That's not fair." Joshua plopped back onto his bed.

Annie inched forward and drew the sheet up to the child's shoulder. "Time to go to sleep, and I'll turn on the night-light."

"Your dad forgot to."

"Did you tell him you like it on?"

"I never do with you. You always just do it."

She shook her head and leaned over to kiss Joshua's forehead. "Good night."

Annie started to stand. Joshua clasped her hand, keeping her sitting on the bed. "Will you read me a story before you go?"

"Sure." Annie usually did. She picked up his favorite book and switched on the light on the nightstand.

Within five minutes Joshua's eyes were

closed. Annie rose, turned the night-light on and the lamp off then headed for the hallway.

"Annie, I love you," Joshua said in a sleepy voice.

Her heart cracked, a pang stabbing her. Emotions swelled inside. Tears threatened.

Annie hurried to give the girls a brief update on the trip and tell them good-night. She needed to escape to her apartment.

After she poked her head into the den to see how Jeremy was doing, she was going to sneak out the sliding glass doors since she heard her father and Ian talking in the kitchen.

"Jeremy, how did it go today?" Annie asked from the doorway.

"Your dad took us fishing. Everyone liked that except Jasmine."

"Did she behave?"

"For a girl."

"No other problems?"

He shook his head, his hand stroking Rex's back.

"See you tomorrow."

As Annie made her way to the breezeway and heard her dad starting his car, she thought of the last time Jeremy had had a seizure—almost two weeks ago. His medication was working much better. That was a relief and would make it easier for her to leave and a new nanny to take over.

As she neared the staircase to her place, she saw a shadow sitting on a step. Charlie? But then the figure rose, and the security light illuminated Ian's face.

"Just checking to make sure you're all right. You fled the kitchen so fast your dad was concerned, and I told him I would look in on you."

"I'm tired of talking and thinking about my scars. I'll be fine tomorrow." *Yeah, right. What makes you think that?*

"Here is Neil's number. When you decide, call him. This is totally up to you. There's no deadline on the offer." Ian came to her and pressed a small sheet of paper into her palm. "Good night."

He turned and strode toward his house.

"Ian."

He stopped but didn't look back.

"Thank you. I appreciate your caring enough to try to fix me."

"I'm not trying to fix you, as you say, but to help you. That's what a person who cares does." He continued forward.

Why had she said it that way? Because that was her conscience talking. Her scars had become a scarlet letter she wore proclaiming her guilt.

* * *

Annie had spent Sunday at church then at her sister's until nightfall. That was the first day in months she hadn't seen Ian or his children at least once. And she was miserable.

Was that why she was rushing to dress this morning, to be at the house when the children woke up? To see Ian before he left for work?

When Annie walked into the kitchen to decide what to fix for breakfast, Ian had a cup of coffee in his hand and was staring out the bay window overlooking the patio and pool. He acknowledged her presence by glancing over his shoulder, then returned to sipping his drink. Since the drive to Dallas a few days before, a barrier stood between her and Ian. Annie had started it, but after that day, he'd added to it. Even the kids noticed. Joshua had said something to her on Saturday about his daddy being mad at her.

After checking the refrigerator for the ingredients for pancakes, she turned toward Ian. "What time will you be home this evening?"

"Early. The agency is sending out a couple of applicants for your job this afternoon. I'd like you to have the children gone from three to five."

"I'm sorry Mary Franklin didn't work out for you."

"She's too young. Barely out of high school. Although I see why you think she'd be good, she doesn't have enough experience."

"Yesterday at church I ran into Mrs. Addison. All the kids in the family she used to work for are in high school. She's been taking a month's break, but now she's ready to move on to a new family. I mentioned you and your children. She's interested."

"Fine. Have her come this afternoon at five with her résumé."

"I'll let her know, and I'll keep the kids away from the house until six."

"Sure." He started for the hallway. "Whatever you think. I'm going to work now."

"But I haven't fixed breakfast yet."

"I'll grab something on the way."

Ian disappeared down the hall. For a moment Annie felt as if a part of herself had walked out of the room. She shook that idea from her mind and concentrated on getting the pancakes ready, then she went to see if the children were up yet.

Later that afternoon when Annie settled on a bench near the playground area at Sooner Park, she felt tired—even after the day of rest on Sunday. Mrs. Addison was arriving at the house at five, so Annie had packed an early dinner for the kids.

She'd have the children eat in a couple of hours. Maybe then she could take her mind off the interviews taking place, especially Mrs. Addison's. She would be perfect for the family, similar to what their aunt had been like. And to satisfy Ian, she wasn't nineteen but in her late forties with a ton of experience, having been a nanny for twenty-five years. He would probably hire her on the spot.

Why am I so depressed by the prospect? I'll be able to leave soon and put my life back on track.

Annie checked her watch over and over, and the hours seemed to crawl by. Keeping an eye on four children required a lot of her concentration, but obviously not enough. All she could think about was leaving in a couple of days.

Jasmine waved to her from the top of the slide while Jade ran toward Annie and plopped on the bench beside her. Jade waved her hand in front of her face. "Hello? Water, please."

Annie dug into the cooler she'd brought and passed a bottle to the young girl. "Having fun?"

"Yes, there are even a couple of friends from school here."

Annie scanned the children, hoping Kayla wasn't one of them. She didn't want Jasmine's afternoon ruined.

"Is Dad joining us for our picnic?"

"No, he has business to take care of. I made him something and left it in the refrigerator."

"He's been upset lately." Jade slanted a look toward her.

Annie tensed. "He must have a lot on his mind."

"Are you going to have the surgery? All of us were wondering. I figured it didn't work out and that made him sad."

Annie had wondered when one of them would ask. "I haven't decided."

"Then, you can have the surgery. Great!" Jade clapped her hands. "But then, why is Dad upset? He was so excited when he went to Dallas with you."

Out of all of Ian's children, Jade was the one who was the hardest to keep anything from. "I can't answer that. You'll have to talk to your dad."

She twisted toward Annie. "Is he mad at you?"

Ian had requested she not say anything about leaving to his kids, and she hadn't. She wouldn't break her word, but looking into Jade's inquisitive expression, she didn't know what to tell the child. She panned the playground again, locating Joshua and Jasmine right away. When Annie couldn't see Jeremy, she stood up. "Just a sec, Jade. Where is Jeremy?"

"He's on the monkey bars."

Annie took a few steps to the right and spied the boy swinging from one end to the other with Rex near him. She sat back on the bench where she had a good view of him.

Jade scooted down to Annie. "You care about us."

Although it wasn't a question, Annie answered, "Yes, of course. You're all special to me." *Then, why am I leaving?*

"Is Dad?"

More than she wanted to admit to Jade—even herself. "Yes."

Jade beamed. "Good." She threw her arms around Annie, kissed her on the cheek then hopped up and raced back to play.

Stunned, Annie touched her cheek. Jade reminded her of herself before the fire: sports oriented and full of life. But the fire had changed her in more ways than physical.

Rex trotted toward her and sat in front of Annie, whining. She glanced at Jeremy still hanging from the monkey bars. "Is something wrong?"

Rex barked.

Annie jumped to her feet. Rex had done this before, and Jeremy had had a seizure not long after. She hurried to the boy. The dog ran to Jeremy and barked insistently. The boy peered at Rex, then Annie and let go of the bar, dropping to the ground.

"Sit on the grass for a few minutes and play with Rex," Annie instructed.

"But I wanted to do the big slide next. Why is he barking?"

"I'm not sure, but I think he senses something. If that's the case, being on the grass would be safer for you."

"But—"

"Please, Jeremy."

With his forehead wrinkled, he trod out of the pool of small, round pebbles under the playground equipment and sank to the lush grass. "How long do I have to stay here?"

"I'm not sure. Awhile." Annie took a seat next to him and checked the ground to make sure there were no objects in the vicinity that could hurt Jeremy.

Jeremy lay back on the grass and began playing with Rex. Within a few minutes, he stiffened and began shaking. She turned him on his side and swiveled her attention between him and his siblings. Rex placed himself right next to Jeremy and licked his face. Sixty seconds later the boy became aware of his surroundings and put his arm around the dog.

"You okay?" Annie relaxed.

He nodded, still dazed a bit. "How did he

know?" Jeremy asked when he sat up and petted Rex.

"The more he is around you, the better he's getting at sensing stuff. There's a connection between you two."

"Good boy. I love you, Rex." Jeremy buried his face against the dog's neck.

A lump in her throat made it difficult for Annie to say anything. Seeing the boy and dog together lifted her spirits. She'd set out to help Jeremy especially, and now he had some help. He wasn't alone.

But I am.

After interviewing two disappointing candidates for the nanny position, Ian sat across from Mrs. Addison. On paper she looked good, but…

She isn't Annie.

Ian had tried to help Annie, and instead she was running away as though she had to pay for her innocent mistake the rest of her life. It broke his heart, but he knew he couldn't force her to accept the truth. Now he needed a nanny to replace Annie, but so far no one had come close to her.

"Do you have any questions about the job, Mrs. Addison?"

"Annie had nothing but good things to say

about you as an employer. I'm not sure why she's leaving, but this job sounds like a nice match for me. I had a nephew with epilepsy and know how to deal with a seizure. I didn't realize dogs could help with them. I'll have to tell my sister about that. Do you have any more questions for me?"

"No, you've given me all the information I need. And your references are impressive." Tired of the process, Ian pushed to his feet. "I'll let you know after I finish my interviewing."

Mrs. Addison clutched her purse and rose. "I'd hoped I could meet your children, but it's awfully quiet in the house."

"They went on a picnic with Annie." Ian glanced at his watch and noted they'd be home soon. He wanted to make sure the candidate was gone before then. He started toward the foyer.

Mrs. Addison followed. "I look forward to hearing from you, Mr. McGregor."

After he shut the door on his last applicant of the day, Ian wanted to bang his head against the wood. He didn't want to do this again. He never thought he would fall in love after Zoe's death. She'd been his life for years, and they'd been happy. Then her being wrenched from his arms had left him shocked for months, really years, until Annie had popped into his life and shaken it up. Shaken his whole family up.

Earlier Ian noticed that Annie had left him a plate with a sandwich and fruit salad. He went into the kitchen, took the food from the refrigerator, sat at his large table and ate. The silence taunted him. As he ate his chicken salad on rye, he stared at the schedule that Annie had put up to help the family keep activities straight. Something that simple had been an enormous aid for him and even the children. When he glimpsed the dogs' water and food bowls, he grinned at the difference Rex and Daisy had made in everyone's life, but especially Jeremy's. Ian had his eldest son back, and he had Annie to thank for that, too.

The sound of the utility room door opening and then footsteps pounding proclaimed his family had returned. Annie was back. For a second his heartbeat raced, then he remembered she would be leaving soon. He ate the last bite and headed for the sink as they all poured into the kitchen.

The first thing Joshua said was "Where's Daisy?"

"Out in the backyard." Ian gestured in that direction. Annie hadn't come in.

"Annie went to her apartment and said she'd be back in a few minutes. Dad, next time we need to take Daisy, too," Jade said while Joshua and Jasmine ran out the back door.

"Someone will have to keep up with her on a leash the whole time."

"We can take turns." Jade walked through the kitchen to the hallway.

"How did it go with you and Rex?" Ian asked Jeremy, who was feeding his dog.

"I had a seizure, but I'm okay now. It wasn't long, and Rex knew about it before it happened." Jeremy straightened from filling Rex's bowl with dry dog food.

"How do you know Rex knew about it?"

"He went and got Annie. She had me sit on the grass. Good thing because I was swinging on the monkey bars." Jeremy talked about the incident as though it was nothing out of the ordinary.

"How long ago?"

His son shrugged. "Probably two hours."

"How did the other kids at the park react?"

"Fine. A couple wanted to know about Rex, and I told them what he did. They were amazed."

And so was he. Ian knew some service dogs noticed a seizure coming on. In a short time Rex and Jeremy had become close. They did everything together, and Jeremy loved having his dog tag along.

Within minutes Rex wolfed down his food,

and he followed Jeremy to the den. Ian thought back to when Jeremy had fought him about having a service dog. A lot had changed.

And the woman coming into the kitchen had been instrumental in it.

"How did the interviews go?" Annie asked after looking around for any children.

"They all showed up."

"Wasn't Mrs. Addison great? The kids at church love her. She teaches a third-and fourth-grade Sunday-school class."

"She was nice."

"That's all? Did you hire her?"

"No, I didn't hire anyone today."

"But you're going to call her back and ask her, aren't you?"

Ian plowed his fingers through his hair. He hadn't thought much about it until Annie had brought it up. If he could avoid...

"Ian?" Annie stepped a few feet closer.

Too near. "I'm not going to hire any of the women tonight."

"What was wrong with Mrs. Addison?"

"Too old."

"First Mary was too young, and now Mrs. Addison is too old. I can't believe it. Either would be a great nanny." She opened her mouth to say more, then closed it.

"My kids are active. I know there are days

you get tired. I certainly do. Keeping up with them requires an experienced hand."

"Between what ages?"

"Twenty-five and forty."

The back door opened, and Jasmine and Joshua came inside with Daisy. Annie glared at Ian while Jasmine fed the dog.

Joshua remained. "Daisy was so happy to see me." Then, as if he sensed the tension in the kitchen, he looked between Ian and Annie. "What's wrong?"

"Nothing you need to worry about, son. We'll be in my office. Jeremy is in the den." Ian walked into the hallway, glancing back to make sure Annie was coming, too.

When he reached his office, he leaned against his desk, too agitated to sit. He clasped its edge and waited for Annie's response.

After shutting the door, she pivoted. "What are you doing? You've turned down two perfectly good nannies. Are you doing this to keep me here?"

Anger surged through him. Ian gritted his teeth and waited to calm down before he answered. "I'm looking out for my children's best interests. What are you afraid of, Annie? Loving a man?"

"Why do you want to change me?"

"Why are you blaming yourself for your mother's death when no one else does?"

She gasped, her eyes wide. "That's low. That isn't something I share with others."

"But you did with me. Why?"

She started to say something but shook her head.

"Annie, it's because you feel something for me beyond employer/employee and even friendship."

"But you don't think I'm good enough for you the way I am."

Ian shoved off the desk and closed the space between them. "That is not why I contacted my friend. If you choose not to have the surgery, that's your decision, and I'll respect it."

"You say that, but when I told you I didn't want it, you went to your friend without my knowledge. So obviously my appearance bothers you more than you'll admit, maybe even to yourself. You're a plastic surgeon—you want people to be as beautiful as possible."

For a moment her words halted him. His mind went blank. Was she right? Not a chance. "Annie, I don't see your scars. I see you. I started caring before I even knew about your scars."

"I don't believe you. You're lying to yourself, Ian. And I think my staying would only complicate the situation. Believe me, I don't want to leave your children. They mean a lot to me."

"Obviously not enough to stay. This will devastate them." *And me.*

"That's why I wanted someone like Mary or Mrs. Addison to take my place."

"No one can do that. I think you're scared. Acknowledging your feelings for me means you can't move on in a few years like you've been doing. You've always been able to put a certain distance between you and the family. You're afraid to give love a chance."

"That isn't true." Annie stiffened, her fists curling and uncurling at her side. "Ian, I'm giving you my two weeks' notice."

Kneading his neck, Ian tried to quash the hurt and pain that filled every part of him. "I think it's best, then, for my children not to come to depend on you any more than they already do. You can leave right away, if that suits you."

Looking stunned, Annie whirled around and threw open the door as she stormed from the office.

Ian started after her but stopped in his tracks when Jasmine and Jade blocked the entrance, horror on their faces. Behind them were Jeremy and Joshua. *They must have heard everything we said.*

* * *

Somehow Annie held back the tears as she drove to the church. She had stopped at Amanda's house, but no one had answered. She needed a refuge in which to think and decide what to do next. She needed the Lord to comfort her, guide her.

Annie noticed some cars in the parking lot, but she prayed no one was in the sanctuary. When she entered the church, she found a pew in front but off to the side, shrouded in shadows.

For a long moment she sat silently. Then emotions flooded her, and she quietly cried. She wasn't yet ready to say goodbye to the children—she wanted to make the transition to a new nanny as easy as possible—but Ian had told her to leave *now.*

If that suits you.

Those words made her pause. Ian had tried to keep her. She'd been the one who'd insisted on going. Tension prickled from her neck down her spine. When she massaged her tight muscles, she felt the rough texture of her scars.

Mom, I miss you so much. I could use your words of wisdom right now. Help me.

"Annie, are you all right? I saw you come into the foyer and waved."

She turned tear-filled eyes on Emma, who stood a few feet from her.

Ian gathered the children in the den on the couch and sat across from them.

"Why is Annie leaving us?" Jasmine asked, then burst into sobs.

Jade held her twin and patted her back. "I thought Annie loved being here. What did we do wrong?"

"It's me. I drove her away with my seizure today. I didn't mean to have it at the park," Jeremy said sadly.

Joshua remained quiet, staring at his lap, then he looked up. "I'll do everything Annie wants if she'll stay."

"Who are Mary and Mrs. Addison?" Jade asked.

"Two women I interviewed to take Annie's place."

"How could you?" Jasmine shot to her feet and ran from the room.

Jeremy moved to the floor in front of the couch and held Rex. Joshua joined him.

"Fix this, Dad," Jade said fiercely.

Ian's desire to fix the family was what had started this. That and making the mistake of falling in love with Annie. "I wish I could."

"There's no choice. You have to."

How do I make someone fall in love with me when she's decided she's not worthy of love?

"May I sit with you?" Emma asked, and took a seat next to Annie before she could answer. "I feel as though we've gotten to know each other lately with Rex. I hate to see someone in pain. I felt as though I needed to come in here and see you. What's wrong?"

For a long moment Annie couldn't even find the words. She'd have to tell Emma everything, even about the fire. When Annie began explaining about her scars, it flowed from her like a flood.

"So what I'm hearing is that you blame yourself for your mother's death."

"I *was* at fault."

"Okay, let's say what you did led to your mom dying."

Her throat full of unshed tears, Annie nodded.

"You think you need to spend the rest of your life paying for that mistake?"

"Yes."

"Why? Who said that? Certainly not the Lord."

"What do you mean?"

"I saw how you were with the McGregor children. You have a gift and a lot of love inside you. God sent you there when they needed you most."

"You've been talking to Amanda."

"Yes, I wanted some background so I could help Jeremy and Rex bond."

Annie folded her hands together and rubbed the back of one.

"You've spent fourteen years mourning your mother's death and keeping yourself apart from others emotionally. I don't believe God asked you to do that. I think you decided you had to without asking Him."

"How can you say that?"

"Because I did the same thing. When my first husband died, I blamed myself. I was the reason he was on the ladder he fell from. My husband now, Jake, helped me to see the error of my thinking. It's okay to forgive yourself, Annie. God did a long time ago. That's the beauty with Him. All we have to do is ask Him from our hearts."

It sounds so easy. But I know it isn't.

"Do you have feelings for Ian?"

"Yes. I haven't let myself feel anything for a long time. I don't..."

"Embrace them. They are a gift from the Lord. He wants you to be happy."

Was that possible?

* * *

When Annie returned to Ian's house, it was ablaze with lights, a beacon in the dark. The kids were usually in bed by now. Had Jeremy had a bad seizure? She hurried through the breezeway and into the utility room and kitchen. Her heartbeat pounded a mad staccato against her rib cage. She charged into the hallway, paused to check the den. Empty.

At Ian's office she peeked in and saw him sitting in his chair, staring at his desktop. The forlorn expression on his face rent her heart into pieces.

"Is something wrong? Jeremy? One of the other children?"

Ian peered up at her, and he erased the look from his face. "I didn't hear you come in. The kids are okay. I need to go up and tell them good-night, but I don't know how much sleep they'll get."

"They overheard us?"

He nodded.

"I'm sorry. I wish they hadn't."

"Oh, well, they needed to know, and I would have stewed over how to tell them." Ian sat forward, resting his elbows on the tan blotter. "Have you decided to leave now?"

Annie heard defeat in his voice. Without

saying a word, she strode to him and leaned against the desk next to him. He swiveled his chair to look at her.

"I've decided to leave—never."

He blinked.

"How can I leave the man I've fallen in love with? Especially when he told me he loved me?"

For a few seconds Ian's face was blank, and then a grin broke through. "You aren't joking, are you?"

"Never about something this important. Ian, you've been right all along. I didn't think I had a right to be happy. I was afraid of feeling anything good. But I love you and the children. I can't imagine my life without you."

Ian jumped to his feet and drew her into an embrace. "You're sure?"

"I went to my church, talked with Emma and came away feeling like a new woman. God forgave me long ago. I just had to forgive myself. If I didn't, I would be hurting a lot of people I care about—including you, your family and mine."

Ian put his hand on her cheek. "Annie, I don't care what you decide about the surgery."

"I believe you."

Ian bent his head toward her and kissed the scars on her neck and cheek, then trailed more to her mouth. When he stopped he said, “This has been the worst and best day of my life. I won’t let you forget how much you mean to me, Annie.”

“Let’s go tell the children. I have to make everything right with them.”

Ian looked over Annie’s shoulder and laughed. “I don’t think you have to.”

All four children along with two dogs poured into the room and surrounded her and Ian with laughter and hugs. *I’ve finally found what I always wanted. Thank You, God.*

Epilogue

"Shh. They're here. Hide."

Coming down the hall, Annie heard Jeremy's words a few seconds before she and Ian entered the den. "I guess my sister hasn't brought them home yet," she said, playing along with the kids wanting to surprise them by hiding.

Ian wrapped his arms around Annie. "Hmm. That gives us more alone time. What do you think we should do?" He kissed her loudly on the mouth.

"Yuck," Jeremy said while the other children, along with Amanda, jumped up and said, "Surprise!"

Jeremy had to help Annie's sister stand up. She was eight months pregnant and big. As Amanda waddled toward them, the children swarmed Ian and Annie, all wanting to know about the honeymoon. Ian actually blushed, then told them about the places they'd visited in Key West.

Amanda hugged Annie then whispered in her ear, "You look great. I see married life agrees with you."

Annie pulled back, chuckling. "How were the kids?"

"Perfect, except..."

Everyone looked at Amanda.

"Except what?" Ian asked.

"They threw me a baby shower."

Annie settled her hands on her waist. "You did that without me?" She tried to look angry.

"It was a trial run," Jasmine said. "We're gonna do another one next week with everyone, including you."

"That is if the baby doesn't come early." Amanda laid her hand over her stomach.

"He'd better not. I have my last laser treatment next week in Dallas. I can't miss the baby's birth." Annie snuggled into the crook of Ian's arm, so glad she'd finally done something about her scars. They were still there, but less obvious, and her prosthetic ear was so realistic looking. But the best part was that Ian had left the decision to her, emphasizing that he thought she was beautiful as she was. Annie knew, without a doubt, he loved her no matter what.

Amanda cleared her throat. "Kids, let's go in the kitchen and get dinner ready."

"But—" Joshua sputtered to a stop because Jade had put her hand over his mouth.

"We're gonna help Amanda. All of us, Joshua." Jade tugged on her brother's arm, pulling him toward the hallway.

After the children left with Amanda, Ian went to the den doorway, looked up and down the hallway then shut the door. "That's just in case they decide to eavesdrop again."

Annie nestled within his embrace. "Our kids don't eavesdrop. They told me they were just keeping themselves informed about what was going on in the family." *My new family.*

Ian kissed the tip of her nose, then settled his mouth over hers, pressing her against him. When he nibbled her ear, she shivered.

"I love you, Mrs. McGregor."

Annie leaned back slightly and looked up at him, running her fingers through his hair. "I might have been a little slow to grasp that, but I know now. And I love you." She pulled his head down so she could kiss him again.

* * * * *

Dear Reader,

The Nanny's New Family is the fourth book in the Caring Canines miniseries. In this story, I dealt with epilepsy, and how the hero copes with the fact that his eldest son has the disorder. As a teacher, I used to work with children who had seizures. I was surprised at what a service dog could do to help a person who has seizures. They are truly amazing animals.

I love hearing from readers. You can contact me at margaretdaley@gmail.com or at PO Box 2074, Tulsa, OK 74101. You can also learn more about my books at margaretdaley.com. I have a newsletter that you can sign up for on my website.

Best wishes,

Margaret Daley